THE TWELVE APOSTLES

Recent Titles by Anthea Fraser

The Detective Chief Inspector Webb Mysteries
(in order of appearance)

A SHROUD FOR DELILAH
A NECESSARY END
PRETTY MAIDS ALL IN A ROW
DEATH SPEAKS SOFTLY
THE NINE BRIGHT SHINERS
SIX PROUD WALKERS
THE APRIL RAINERS
SYMBOLS AT YOUR DOOR
THE LILY-WHITE BOYS
THREE, THREE, THE RIVALS
THE GOSPEL MAKERS
THE SEVEN STARS
ONE IS ONE AND ALL ALONE
THE TEN COMMANDMENTS
ELEVEN THAT WENT UP TO HEAVEN *
THE TWELVE APOSTLES *

Other Titles

PRESENCE OF MIND *
THE MACBETH PROPHECY *
BREATH OF BRIMSTONE *
MOTIVE FOR MURDER *
DANGEROUS DECEPTION *

* *available from Severn House*

THE
TWELVE
APOSTLES

Anthea Fraser

This first world edition published in Great Britain 1999 by
SEVERN HOUSE PUBLISHERS LTD of
9–15 High Street, Sutton, Surrey SM1 1DF.
First published in the USA 2000 by
SEVERN HOUSE PUBLISHERS INC., of
595 Madison Avenue, New York, NY 10022.

British Library Cataloguing in Publication Data

Fraser,   Anthea
        The twelve apostles
        1.   Webb, Chief Inspector (Fictitious character) - Fiction
        2.   Police - Fiction
        3.   Detective and mystery stories
        1.   Title
        823.9'14 [F]

        ISBN 0-7278-5494-1

Typeset by Hewer Text Ltd
Edinburgh, Scotland.
Printed and bound in Great Britain by
MPG Books Ltd, Bodmin, Cornwall.

Green Grow the Rushes-O

I'll sing you one-O!
(*Chorus*) Green grow the rushes-O!
  What is your one-O?
One is one and all alone and evermore shall be so.

I'll sing you two-O!
(*Chorus*) Green grow the rushes-O!
  What are your two-O?
Two, two, the lily-white Boys, clothed all in green-O,
(*Chorus*) One is one and all alone and evermore shall be so.

I'll sing you three-O!
(*Chorus*) Green grow the rushes-O!
  What are your three-O?
Three, three, the Rivals,
(*Chorus*) Two, two, the lily-white Boys, clothed all in green-O.
One is one and all alone and evermore shall be so.

Four for the Gospel-makers.
Five for the Symbols at your door.
Six for the six proud Walkers.
Seven for the seven Stars in the sky.
Eight for the April Rainers.
Nine for the nine bright Shiners.
Ten for the ten Commandments.
Eleven for the Eleven that went up to Heaven.
Twelve for the twelve Apostles.

The Greenwood and Ryder Families

Eva Greenwood, widow of Max
Adam Greenwood, her eldest son, a TV interviewer
Sonia Greenwood, Adam's first wife
William, Bethany and Seb Greenwood, Adam and Sonia's
   children
Imogen Greenwood, Adam's second wife
Mia Perry, Imogen's daughter

Russell Greenwood, Eva's second son, a travel writer and
   TV personality
Louise Greenwood, his wife, daughter of Verity Ryder – see
   below
Tom and Rebecca Greenwood, Louise and Russell's
   children

Elliott Greenwood, Eva's third son, an actor
Margo Devereux, his girlfriend

Verity Ryder, widow of Charles and lifelong friend of Eva
Naomi Ryder, a sculptor, her elder daughter
[Louise Greenwood, Verity's younger daughter – see above]

One

V erity Ryder stood in the centre of the large, handsome room and surveyed the chaos about her – suitcases on the bed spilling out clothes and toiletries, tea chests lined against one wall, cardboard boxes and carrier bags in profusion. The rosewood furniture at least was familiar, and she glanced at it with affection. Like her, it seemed unsure of itself in its new surroundings, as though aware she might yet rearrange it.

Well, I've done it! she told herself, with a mixture of satisfaction and trepidation. She'd surrendered her independence – or most of it – to live her life surrounded by Greenwoods. She wondered what Charles would have made of it.

But Charles had been dead for almost three years now, and desolate, lonely years they'd been. Which was why she'd first contemplated sharing a house with Eva.

Eva Greenwood – or Pride, as she was in the old days – had been her closest friend for over sixty years, since they had met on their first day at infant school. They'd spent teenage holidays together, been each other's bridesmaid and, later, godmother to each other's first child, and the seal had been set when, twenty years ago, Verity's younger daughter Louise had married Eva's second son.

Throughout her life, it seemed, in good times and bad, Eva had always been there. As she still was – just across the landing, in fact.

It had been when they were discussing moving in together, Eva's husband having died some years before Charles, that

1

Russell and Louise proposed their plan. Russell, like all the Greenwoods, thought Verity wryly, was a household name – a travel writer and broadcaster who spent his time visiting exotic places with a camera crew, and later writing books about them and appearing in television series. It was a very lucrative lifestyle.

As it happened, the TV programmes were made at the Shillingham studios, and since they had both grown up in Broadshire, he and Louise decided to move back there. Which was when they'd found Greenwood, and fallen for it.

"Not only because of its name, Mother," Louise had enthused over the phone, "though surely that must be an omen! But it's a really gorgeous house, and *huge* – far too big for just the four of us."

"So why—?"

"Which was when we had our brainwave," Louise hurried on. "It would lend itself perfectly to being divided; one end could be made into a self-contained maisonette and the other into two flats, still leaving loads of room in the middle for us."

"And who," Verity had said into the pause, "are you proposing to install in all this living space?"

"Well, that's the point. We wondered if you and Eva would like to share the maisonette? You could have a really large bedsitter each – en suite, of course – for when you wanted a bit of privacy, and share the kitchen and sitting-cum-dining room downstairs. You said you were thinking of moving in together, and it would be so wonderful to have you both here. And Adam and Elliott could have a flat each as a *pied-à-terre* when they're in the area. A real family house."

A *Greenwood* family house, Verity had amended silently, though her own daughter was one of them. "How does Eva feel about it?" she'd asked cautiously.

"Russ is phoning her today." Pause. "Will you at least let us take you to see it? I'm sure you'll fall for it, just as we did. And you'll be close to Naomi, too," she added with cunning. Naomi was Verity's elder daughter, an unmarried sculptor at present living in Shillingham with a strange young man who claimed to be a poet.

And so, of course, it had gone ahead. Verity walked to the bay window and looked down on the garden, feeling as though she were at the prow of a ship. The house stood on a corner and at some height above the pavement; to her right, Hunter's Hill led all the way down to the town centre, while opposite, in Hampton Rise, other large houses stood at well-spaced intervals.

There was a tap on the door behind her, and Louise appeared with a tray of tea. Tall and slim with a cloud of dark hair, she was dressed in businesslike jeans and sweatshirt, which she wore with the same easy grace as her more usual designer clothes.

"I thought you might welcome a break," she was saying. "Eva wants to carry on for the moment, so I've left hers in her room."

"Oh darling, you've enough to do without bothering about us."

"Don't worry, I've marshalled the troops and we're getting along famously." She set the tray on one of the tables. "Come and sit down for a minute."

Louise studied her mother as Verity moved to join her. The soft hair was as immaculate as always, but the grey eyes had mauve shadows beneath them and to Louise's anxious eyes the tall, slender frame seemed to droop a little. It struck her with a sudden pang that her mother was *old*, and here they were, uprooting her from the home where she'd lived for the last thirty-five years – an experience acknowledged to be one of the most traumatic in life.

"Not having second thoughts, are you?" she asked gently.

She was only half-joking, and Verity, guiltily repressing her doubts, shook her head. "Of course not."

"Or worried about being lost in the greenwood?" Louise persisted with a smile.

"It will be lovely having you and the children so near," Verity said firmly. "And Russell and Eva too, of course." *And after all, Adam and Elliott would be only infrequent visitors.* The thought

3

had come before she could stop it and she bit her lip. It distressed her that although Adam was her godson, she felt less than comfortable with him. But that was her secret, and one she would never betray.

"And the nice thing is that although you're so close, the two of you are completely self-contained," Louise was continuing, "with your separate entrance and everything. I know I came barging in just now – you hadn't put the snip down – but once we're all settled, I wouldn't dream of dropping in unannounced, and I'll see that the kids don't, either."

"My dear girl!" Verity protested, leaning forward to take her cup. "That's not—"

"No, really, it's important. You need your space – we all do."

"Very well, if you say so."

Louise glanced round the room appraisingly. "You'll soon have this looking like home. Thank goodness we were able to absorb so many of your things – and Eva's, too. That must have made it easier, leaving the Oxford house."

Verity nodded. "And I've kept some of the nicer pieces that I hadn't room for; they're in store, in case Tom and Rebecca would like them in due course."

Louise put a hand over her mother's. "I'm sure they would. And talking of my offspring, I'd better go back and see how they're getting on." She stood up. "See you later. You know Russ has booked a table for us all at the King's Head this evening? In the meantime, give me a buzz on the intercom if there's anything you need."

Five minutes later Eva tapped on the door and, at Verity's invitation, came briskly into the room, bringing with her, as she always did, an air of purpose and efficiency. Her hair, dark when she was younger, was now silver – so much prettier, Verity thought, than her own pepper-and-salt – and expertly cut to flatter her still-youthful face. There was no denying that Eva and her late husband had been a handsome couple, and had passed on their good looks in varying degrees to their three sons.

4

"My goodness," she was exclaiming, "you're much farther on than I am. What do you bet that a week from now we'll feel we've never lived anywhere else?"

Her eyes lit on the sheaf of spring flowers temporarily stuck in a water jug. "Oh, how lovely! Where did those come from?"

"Naomi, bless her, with the message *Welcome Home.* She couldn't join us this evening, but she's invited me for lunch on Friday. Lovely to think that after all these years we're near enough for that."

Eva nodded, perching on the arm of a chair. "Adam, Imogen and Mia have arrived; he just buzzed through. They came in convoy with their furniture van – only a small one, Adam says, as they're bringing just the essentials for now, till they can judge how much they need. I've not seen them for a while, but no doubt we'll hear all their news over dinner."

Verity forced a smile and a nod. She would have preferred not to have the company of Adam and his new wife, as she still thought of Imogen, but the die was cast.

"I'm glad he's here," Eva added, picking up an ornament from the mantelshelf and absentmindedly putting it down again. "I think he was more upset than he admitted about that unpleasantness the other week."

Verity murmured an appropriate reply. Adam was a high-powered television interviewer, known for his aggressive and abrasive style which had ruffled more than a few feathers over the years. His programme, *Adam Greenwood Live*, had become compulsive viewing for a large part of the nation, a fact borne out by a recent BAFTA award. A couple of weeks ago there'd been an exceptionally acrimonious encounter, when the man being interviewed – a high-ranking civil servant – had taken exception to the line of questioning to the extent of jumping out of his seat and, in front of millions of viewers, punching Adam on the jaw.

Needless to say, the episode had made the headlines in the national press, with, Verity suspected, a large percentage of readers happy to see Adam Greenwood get what might be termed his come-uppance.

"How long are they staying?" Verity asked. "Will he get a chance to see the family?"

Adam's ex-wife and three children lived locally.

"Oh, didn't I mention it? Now his series has finished for the summer, he's been booked for six 'Regional Specials' here in Shillingham. They start this week, so the timing couldn't be better. Something to do with the town's five-hundredth anniversary. So Mia will be able to go back to school straight from here." Eva smiled. "If it weren't for her luggage, she could have walked it. Very convenient – and especially for Rebecca, of course, since she'll be a day girl. It'll be nice for her to have Mia to show her the ropes."

Verity thought back to the only time she'd met Adam's stepdaughter, at his and Imogen's wedding two years ago, and remembered feeling sorry for the gawky, long-haired schoolgirl. Shortly afterwards, Mia's father also remarried and his wife had since had a baby – which, Verity was sure, would do little to restore the girl's sense of security.

Eva stood up, breaking into her thoughts. "Well, I'm determined to unpack two more tea-chests before I change for dinner, so I'd better be getting back. See you later."

Verity nodded and, levering herself out of the armchair, returned to her own sorting.

The Greenwood table in the King's Head restaurant that evening caused quite a stir, including as it did two famous members of the dynasty seldom seen together in public. Hannah James, headmistress-designate of Ashbourne School for Girls, regarded them from across the room with a jaundiced eye.

"They've moved into the next road up from me," she told her friends, "and for months there've been hordes of workmen milling around with pneumatic drills and bulldozers and Lord knows what. Did you hear they've raised the garden wall to a height of eight feet and installed electronic gates? I'm surprised the planning department sanctioned it."

Gwen Cameron, Ashbourne's present head, grimaced. "Hannah and I should declare our interest," she told the others. "Firstly, Adam Greenwood is doing a quincentennial programme from the school, which is a mixed blessing, and secondly the girl with long hair is his stepdaughter and one of our pupils. Furthermore, the little dark one is Rebecca Greenwood, Russell's daughter, and will be joining us next week."

"I agree about the mixed blessing," Monica Latimer remarked, sipping her wine, "he's coming to us, too." Born Monica Tovey, she was the proprietor of Randall Tovey, Broadshire's leading fashion store.

"But to get back to the girls," Dilys Hayward intervened, "you've had the offspring of the famous before, so what's the problem? You're not thinking of installing electronic gates yourself?"

Gwen laughed. "Hardly. But things do rub off on the children. That fiasco on TV with Adam sent sprawling in his chair, for instance; it caused plenty of talk, as you might imagine, and naturally it was Mia who suffered." She paused. "Actually, I'm a little concerned about her; she's always been a dreamer, but she seems to be withdrawing more and more into herself."

"Have you spoken to her parents?" Monica asked.

Gwen shrugged. "I've tried. But her mother moved to London after her second marriage, leaving Mia to board, which I never thought a good idea. Some children adapt easily to boarding school, but I feared Mia wasn't one of them, and I've been proved right.

"Her mother seems fond enough of her," Gwen added fairly, "but she's caught up in her new life and has only been down to see her once. Mia spends the holidays in London, but goes to her father for exeat weekends – which I think must be a strain. His new wife is only about ten years older than she is, and now there's a baby on the scene which, as babies do, tends to steal the limelight.

"However –" Gwen squared her shoulders – "we're not here to discuss Ashbourne problems, but to celebrate Dilys's new book." She raised her glass. "So here's to massive sales and a lucrative TV deal, Dil, and more power to your elbow!"

And, raising their glasses, the four women dismissed the Greenwoods from their thoughts.

Back in their new flat, Imogen kicked off her shoes and dropped on to the sofa, running her fingers through her short blonde hair.

"So – here we are!"

"Indeed. Can I pour you a nightcap?"

"That'd be lovely."

"Mia gone to bed?"

Imogen nodded. "She likes her room – especially the *en suite* bathroom. I must say, the flat's been very well designed."

She looked approvingly round the large room, decorated in the colour scheme she and Adam had chosen. Patio doors gave on to the garden, now rectangles of blackness, and the furniture they'd brought from London was dotted about somewhat sparsely. However, there were still some items in store which had fallen to her when she and Scott separated – a little bureau, some chairs and a drop-side table, which would fit admirably in the dining alcove. At the moment, a card table, which had been set up as a temporary measure, stood in splendid isolation.

And the kitchen, Imogen thought, though small, was fully fitted with the latest gadgets and would fulfil all their needs for the short spells they'd be staying here.

"I'm glad we went for the ground floor," she said contentedly, taking the glass from her husband. "Access to the garden is a big advantage."

Adam sat down beside her, fingering his still-tender jaw. Even under the concealer Imogen had applied earlier, the purple swelling was discernible.

"Glad you're pleased with it. I must say, moving in was pretty painless – not the mammoth job the rest of them are having. They'll be unpacking tea-chests for weeks."

"Well, this will be their permanent home. When's Elliott putting in an appearance, do you know?"

"Sunday. His current play comes off this week and he's anxious to get things straight before rehearsals start for the Pinter. Fortuitously enough, it's opening with a tour which starts in Bristol and Bath, so he wants the flat ready to avoid having to resort to digs."

"Is Maggie coming with him?" Imogen asked. "On Sunday, I mean?" Elliott was currently living with Margo Devereux, a young actress who was making quite a name for herself.

"He didn't mention her, but I dare say she might, depending on her schedule. Mind you, I reckon a couple of days is the longest she'd stay away from London, Elliott or no Elliott, unless she's on tour herself. One for the bright lights, is our Maggie."

Adam picked up the newspaper they'd brought with them and not had a chance to read.

"Your godmother seemed rather quiet over dinner," Imogen commented as he shook the pages into place.

"Probably tired."

"Unlike your mother."

"Ah well, Ma's a different kettle of fish. She has the stamina of a horse – I hope I've half her energy, at her age." He paused. "I also suspect that dear Verity has her reservations about yours truly."

Imogen raised an eyebrow. "How so?"

"Oh, nothing I could put a finger on. She does her godmotherly duty, and all that, but I get the impression I haven't her full approval. Perhaps," he added sardonically, "her prayers for me haven't been answered in quite the way she hoped!"

He smoothed the newspaper and Imogen, taking the hint, was silent, leaning her head against the cushion and letting her thoughts wander. It would be strange being back in Shillingham

9

for the next six weeks; she hoped she wouldn't run into Scott and Judy. Though the divorce hadn't been too bad all things considered, matters progressed more smoothly if they were conducted politely from a distance rather than face to face.

Adam's exclamation broke into her thoughts. "Good God!"

She sat up, opening her eyes. "What is it? . . . Adam?" she prompted, when he did not reply.

"Greg Blaise has died; he was only my age – I knew him at university. They've given him a full-page obit: 'Sir Gregory Blaise, the well-known brain surgeon, has died at the age of forty-eight after a short illness. The son of—' and so on."

"I've never heard you mention him. Have you seen him lately?"

"No, no, not since we all came down. Nevertheless, when one of your contemporaries kicks the bucket, it gives you quite a jolt."

" 'In the midst of life . . .' " Imogen quoted.

"Oh thanks, that's all I need!"

She leaned over and kissed him contritely on the cheek. "Sorry, darling. Well, I'm ready for bed, but I'm not going to leave you by yourself feeling all morbid, so up you get. You can read the rest in the morning."

And Adam, letting the paper slip to the floor, allowed himself to be pulled to his feet and led out of the room.

Mia heard muted voices in the hallway, followed by the closing of the bedroom door. Her own room, slightly smaller, was at the front, and although the house was set well back from the road, light from a street lamp seeped through the curtains, faintly illuminating the unfamiliar outlines.

She let her mind drift back over the day: the packing at home in Hampstead, including everything she'd need for the summer term; the arrival of the van and loading of the selected items – beds and bedding, sofas and chairs, portable television, china, cutlery and glasses. Then the journey along the M4, stopping for a snack lunch, and finally arriving here and unpacking everything.

She hadn't wanted to go out to dinner, and would have much preferred to curl up on the sofa and watch TV, but Mum wouldn't hear of it. Then, to cap it all, who should have been in the restaurant but her two heads, and she'd suffered agonies of embarrassment every time someone at her table raised their voice or laughed a little too loudly.

The flat was nice, though, especially having her own private bathroom, where she could soak for as long as she liked without anyone banging on the door. Would they let her come here for exeat weekends, she wondered suddenly, instead of going to Dad's? Even when Mum and Adam were in London, there'd be Russell and Louise just through the wall, so she wouldn't be alone. But then, she reminded herself, they weren't her relatives, so couldn't be expected to take responsibility for her.

She did hate going to Coombes Crescent, though, specially since Rosie was born and it was impossible to have an uninterrupted conversation. Judy made an effort, but Mia knew she didn't enjoy having her to stay, and Dad was extra hearty and friendly, which Mia found embarrassing.

The trouble was, she didn't seem to fit in anywhere. At school all the other girls were in groups or pairs and she was the odd one out. And since Mum and Dad had split she'd felt an outsider in both homes, sure they'd rather be alone with their new partners.

Her throat tightened with self-pity. It would save them all a lot of hassle if she simply ran away and found herself a job somewhere, she told herself rebelliously. Then they could stop feeling guilty about her.

She sat up, thumped her pillow fiercely, and lay down again. Then a memory surfaced which brought with it a morsel of comfort; during dinner she had several times caught the eye of Tom Greenwood – who, she supposed, would be her stepcousin – and once he had given her a deliberate wink.

At the time, she'd been so conscious of her headmistresses

across the room that she'd barely registered him. Now, though, she smiled sleepily in the darkness and settled herself more comfortably. Any hint of interest was balm to her bruised ego, and despite her previous angst she drifted off to sleep with the smile still on her lips.

Earlier that evening, some thirty-five miles north-west of Shillingham and just short of the Gloucestershire border, Marilyn Piper, aged fifteen, walked in the woods with her sixteen-year-old boyfriend.

"I must get back," she said for the third time. "Mum'll kill me – I have to be in by ten, and it's half-nine now. She thinks I'm at Tracey's, and if I'm late she'll phone her mum."

"There's loads of time," Wayne told her, pulling her into his arms and nuzzling her neck. His breath was warm in her ear and she gave a little shudder of excitement, half fearful, half anticipatory, as he pulled her to the ground, soft and rustling with last year's fallen leaves.

But barely a minute later, as the pressure of his hands grew more demanding, her response faded and renewed anxiety took its place.

"No, really," she began, rolling away from him, "we must—" and broke off with a little cry as she landed on something hard.

"What's wrong? Ah, come on, Marilyn—"

But she was sitting up, rubbing her shoulder. "Something dug into me. It didn't half hurt."

"Must be a root or a bit of stone. Look, don't go yet; we've plenty of time, and it won't take long to get back if we put a spurt on."

But Marilyn wasn't listening. Running her hand over the ground beside her, she gave a satisfied exclamation and held up an object some eight inches long, grey in the dim evening light.

"Looks like a bone," Wayne said dismissively, annoyed that his lovemaking had been so summarily rejected. "Some dog must have buried it."

12

Marilyn frowned, her fingers again moving uncertainly among the leaves. "Here's another – oh, God!" She sprang to her feet, frantically wiping her hand down her skirt as though to rid it of contamination.

Alarmed, Wayne leaned over to look. And realised, as she had, that this was not one bone but several joined together, forming the unmistakable shape of a human hand.

Their eyes met, wide, questioning and frightened. Then Wayne caught hold of her arm and the two of them started to run, racing back the way they had come, stumbling over the uneven ground, torn at by trailing brambles, gasping for breath, but not slackening their pace until they were clear of the woods and out in the open countryside. Then with one accord they stopped, bending over, hands on knees, until their lungs stopped pumping and their breathing became more even.

"Do you think," Marilyn asked unsteadily, "that the – the rest of it was there?"

"Search me. We should tell the police or someone."

She caught frantically at his arm. "We *can't*, Wayne! We can't let anyone know we were *in the wood*! Mum'd—"

"Kill you," Wayne finished heavily. "Yeah, you said. But we could make an anonymous—"

"No, we *couldn't*! They can always be traced. Then the police'd come round and we'd have to say how we came to find it, that we were – lying down, and everything."

"That's all we were doing," Wayne said bitterly.

"We shouldn't have been there, anyway. Wayne, *promise* me you won't tell anyone?"

He hesitated. He fancied Marilyn, and despite this evening's setback, reckoned he was in with a chance – as long as he didn't blow it by upsetting her. Anyway, he told himself, it wasn't as if they'd found a *new* body. This one must have been there for years – no one would be looking for whoever it was any more. And now they'd uncovered the bones, someone else would be sure to see them, then *they* could do the necessary.

"All right," he said grudgingly, "I promise." And silently, hand in hand, they began walking through the darkening fields towards the safety of their homes.

Two

During the next two days, the house gradually became less like a refugee centre; boxes were unpacked, removed, and their contents salted away in new locations; the last of the curtains were hung, pictures put up and ornaments set out, and in the maisonette Verity and Eva settled into their new routine.

Both were pleased with the downstairs sitting room, which contained furniture from each of their homes. The curtains and carpet were new, but Verity's terracotta armchairs looked good alongside Eva's buttermilk sofa, and Eva's small round dining table was of the same wood as Verity's bookcase. The room, they both agreed, was attractive, comfortable and welcoming, and they already felt at home there.

They'd agreed from the outset that they would be entirely independent; if one of them were invited out with friends or family, there was no question of feeling she should invite the other along. Nevertheless, it seemed reasonable that, if nothing else was on, they should share their evening meal, and already they were enjoying the company and looking forward to talking over with each other the happenings of the day.

Breakfast, however, was taken separately, Eva settling at the kitchen bar with a boiled egg and the morning paper, Verity preferring tea and toast in her room, as had been her custom for years. On the Thursday morning, Eva came into the kitchen as Verity was making toast.

"Adam's first programme goes out tonight," she remarked,

filling a pan with water, "and he's been given a clutch of tickets. Would you like to come?"

Verity hesitated. "I wouldn't want to butt in—"

"No question of that," Eva said briskly. "The children aren't interested, but Louise, Russell, Imogen and I are going." She smiled. "Adam'll get a taste of his own medicine tonight; to start off the series, he's being interviewed himself – allegedly about growing up in Shillingham, but really as a plug for the rest of the programmes, which will come from different venues around the town."

"It should be interesting," Verity said dutifully. "Thanks, I'd like to come." She could only hope no one here would take it into their heads to attack Adam. That was both the excitement and the anxiety of live programmes; quite apart from the much-publicised fracas, incidents had often occurred or words been spoken which, had chance offered, would have been edited out before transmission.

"Fine," Eva said, dropping an egg into the now boiling water. "We'll be leaving at eight – there are drinks first in the hospitality suite."

Nigel Packard, barefoot and wrapped in a less than clean towelling robe, hitched himself on to the corner of the table and took the mug of coffee Naomi handed him.

The local paper, open beside him, carried an article about the forthcoming television series.

"So tell me about these Greenwoods," he said, holding the mug in both hands and gingerly sipping the steaming liquid. "All very high profile, aren't they? They must be rolling in it."

"I suppose they must," Naomi agreed. "I've never really thought about it; they're just people I've known all my life."

"And your sister married one of them. Missed out there, didn't you?"

Naomi flushed. She was quite fond of Nigel, but he had this habit of making slightly malicious comments which she found hurtful. "Russell isn't my type," she said lightly, "but he makes a very good brother-in-law."

"Well, go on, then; how did it all start, this palliness?"

"With Mother and Eva – they were at school together and have been friends ever since. When we were children, we all went on holiday together."

"What did Pa Greenwood do?"

"Max? He was a naturalist; wrote definitive books on fungi, carnivorous plants, orchids, and so on. He used to broadcast, too – radio, though, not television."

"And you all lived here in Shillingham?"

"The Greenwoods did; my parents moved to Steeple Bayliss when they married, because my father was a lecturer at the university. Then he was offered a post at Oxford, so we went there. That was where Louise and I grew up, and where my mother continued to live until this week."

"And the others stayed on here?" Nigel persisted.

"No, they eventually moved to London, but by that time Adam was married to his first wife, Sonia, who was a Shillingham girl. When they split up she moved back with the children, to be near her parents. And oddly enough his second wife comes from here, too. They met through mutual friends."

Naomi sipped her own coffee and Nigel watched her, as he often did. She had a lovely face, he thought dispassionately, with fantastic bone structure, but she took no interest in her appearance. Though pale, she never used make-up and her long brown hair, fastened with a slide at the neck, hung down her back in a style he considered too young for her. She was in fact nearly ten years his senior, but she'd been good to him, offering him board and lodging and occasionally her bed, though he accepted that it was his work rather than his body that interested her.

Had he but known it, Naomi was regarded by her family as a collector of lame ducks, and a soft touch for any struggling artist, be he – or, to be fair, she – poet, painter or musician.

"And that actor guy is another of them?"

17

"Elliott? Yes, he's the youngest by several years – an after-thought, as they say." She looked at him, frowning a little. "Why the sudden interest in the Greenwoods?"

"Because you can't bloody move without hearing or reading about them, and because until now I hadn't realised you knew them."

Naomi shrugged. "No reason why you should." She rinsed her mug under the tap and up-ended it on the draining board. "Incidentally, my mother's coming for lunch tomorrow."

"Which, translated, means make myself scarce." His voice held the resentful tone which was increasingly beginning to grate on her.

"If you would."

"And tidy my room before I go, in case Mummy wants to look round the flat?"

"That's enough, Nigel!" Naomi spoke sharply, and saw that she'd surprised him.

"All right, all right," he said placatingly, "only joking. You can take a joke, can't you?"

She didn't answer. Slipping off the table, he lifted the tail of brown hair and kissed her neck, warm above the flowered kimono.

She shrugged free of him. "Oh, grow up. I'm going to have a shower, then I want to finish that bust. What are you doing today?"

He shrugged morosely.

She turned to look at him, shaggy and bearded, his black hair uncombed. No, Mother wouldn't approve, she thought with a touch of amusement, but then she ran her life to suit herself, not her mother, and if Nigel outstayed his welcome or continued to annoy her, she was quite capable of giving him his marching orders.

She watched him unwrap a half-eaten Easter egg, biting back a reproof as flakes of chocolate fell to the floor. She mustn't ride him too hard; after all, he had a genuine gift if he would

18

only settle down and work at it. And she could wash the floor later.

Leaving him munching, she went for her shower.

The town of Shillingham was *en fête*, an ongoing celebration scheduled to last throughout the year. Flags flew above shop fronts, acrobats and jugglers performed, and in the warm spring sunshine people sat at pavement cafés, drinking in the atmosphere as avidly as the coffee. Above all the hubbub, it was possible now and again to catch snatches of music from the band playing in Central Gardens. Life would seem very flat, thought Sonia Greenwood, when everything reverted to normal.

Meanwhile, as she had good reason to know, the local schools were vying with each other in the number of concerts, plays and sporting events they could fit in, and she seemed to have spent an unconscionable time lately clapping and cheering the efforts of her offspring. However, the schools' main contribution to the festivities was scheduled for a month's time, when they were combining to take part in a pageant entitled Shillingham Through the Ages. As usual, parents had been coerced into making the costumes, which was why, instead of returning home when she'd finished work at lunchtime, she was here in the thick of it, fighting the crowds.

Not, Sonia admitted honestly, that it had been essential to come down today; the truth was that she'd avoided going home in case Adam phoned. Better by far that he and the children make their own arrangements to meet without involving her. Even knowing he was in the vicinity unsettled her, which, as she freely admitted, was pathetic.

They'd been apart for four years now. Until the divorce came through he had lived with Imogen Perry, while Sonia nursed the secret hope that he might tire of her, abandon the proceedings and come home. Instead, he and Imogen had married and, like a wounded animal, Sonia returned to her roots, bringing her three children with her.

Their marriage, she reflected, had been many things: tumultuous, stimulating, wonderful, frustrating and, finally, unbearable – but never, never dull. Amazing, really, to think she'd held on to selfish, opinionated Adam for sixteen years. Even more amazing that she still loved him.

However, that was all water under the bridge, and the only ripples nowadays were when he made his periodic visits to Broadshire. The rest of them, meanwhile, had settled down to their new lives, Sonia as part-time receptionist at a busy group practice, William, now nineteen, reading media studies – what else? – at a college near Swindon.

Of the younger two, Bethany, in her final year at Shillingham High, was planning to go on to drama school. Those Greenwood genes, Sonia thought with some bitterness, had certainly swamped her own.

And Seb, at fifteen, was at the grammar school and so far, thank God, had not voiced any career preferences. It was for Bethany and Seb that she had now to produce costumes, Plantagenet and Victorian respectively, heaven help her.

She turned into a department store in search of end-of-roll bargains, doubtfully fingering velvet and hessian as she considered their appropriateness to the sketches the schools had supplied. With luck, Seb might get away with school uniform, plus a stovepipe hat made out of cardboard and a wing collar. And, she thought, interest belatedly stirring, she could tack on some of this black material to give the effect of a frock coat.

She glanced at her watch. One thirty. Had Adam phoned? William would be going back to Swindon on Monday and didn't always come home at weekends; if Adam wanted to see him, he had better not delay.

She made a sudden, impatient movement. Damn it, she would *not* spend her time worrying about her ex-husband, who usually got what he wanted, anyway. Determinedly closing her mind to him, Sonia decided to buy the black material and some velvet, and, calling the assistant over, concentrated on the task in hand.

* * *

At eight fifteen a train drew into Shillingham station and a small, elderly man in the front carriage folded his newspaper with a sigh; he was not looking forward to the next couple of hours. The train shuddered noisily to a halt and the man remained seated while his fellow passengers retrieved their belongings from the racks and jostled their way towards the doors. He had no luggage other than his briefcase, and he was not in a hurry.

Finally, when the carriage had emptied, he rose to his feet, stepped down on to the platform and made his way to the taxi rank. His tardiness had ensured there was a queue in front of him and he waited patiently until his turn came.

"The television studios, please."

His date with destiny, he thought as the driver, with an uninterested nod, started up the engine. Then, with heavy heart, he settled back and resigned himself to whatever lay ahead.

Verity had never been in a television studio before, and was fascinated to recognise sets which were familiar to her from progammes she had seen. Not that she'd time to study them, because Russell had taken her arm and was whisking her along after the rest of them in the direction of the hospitality suite.

Voices and laughter came to meet them down the length of a long corridor, and she wondered who else had benefited from Adam's 'clutch' of tickets.

Which of them, other than the family, were his personal guests Verity did not discover, but judging by the people to whom she was introduced, all the great and the good of Shillingham appeared to be here – the mayor, town councillors, heads of the various schools and colleges, and, most interesting of all, the conductor Sir Julian Harwood and his wife, who turned out to be near neighbours.

"Wasn't his sister the composer who died in a plane crash?" Verity murmured to Eva as the Harwoods moved away.

"That's right, her equal claim to fame being that after her death it was discovered she'd been a serial killer. Sir Julian promptly had a heart attack, for which you can't blame him, but his career hasn't suffered and he's on top form again now."

"What interesting lives some people lead!" Verity said drily, and Eva gave her irrepressible chuckle.

"Who in particular, Mamma?" enquired Louise, who had come up in time to hear the remark.

"No one you know, darling," Verity answered serenely. "Do you think you could find me some more of that delicious smoked salmon? The waiter didn't come near us on his last round."

"He must have seen the predatory gleam in your eye," Louise said severely, "and decided to let other people have a look-in. OK, I'll see what I can do."

Verity glanced at her friend, noting the tightness round her jaw. "Not nervous, are you, on behalf of your first-born?"

Eva met her eye. "A little, though I wouldn't admit it to anyone else. I'm always afraid he'll say the wrong thing, or simply put it badly, and then everyone will leap on him – figuratively, I trust – and it will be all over the press."

"He'd be the first to say there's no bad publicity."

"I don't happen to agree. I suffer agonies whenever he's on the box. Usually at least I'm in the privacy of my own home and can have smelling salts or whatever to hand, but here I'll be on public view, with everyone watching to see how I react."

Verity laid her hand lightly on Eva's arm. "Poor love, I'd no idea you took it so much to heart. You didn't have to come, you know."

"Of course I did."

"Who's interviewing him?"

"Gregory Page, I believe."

"Good heavens, Adam could eat him for breakfast."

"If he were in the chair, yes. How he'll fare on the receiving end remains to be seen."

Louise returned with a waiter in tow bearing a platter of smoked salmon, and Verity had just time to take a couple of morsels before they were all rounded up and escorted to the studio.

The Greenwood party was seated in the front row, where some of the glare and heat from the lights spilled over them. Verity began to realise what Eva'd meant about being on show.

A lot of technical discussion was going on between the director, high in his control box, and the floor manager, wearing headphones and carrying a script board as he bustled about supervising last-minute adjustments to the set. Meanwhile, engineers were checking the lighting and carrying out sound-balance tests on the microphones.

Eventually, the floor manager turned his attention to the audience, explaining that as their participation made an important contribution to the programme, they should feel free to respond and laugh at any time – and he would be signalling them to applaud at appropriate moments by clapping his hands above his head. Verity wondered if the man had ever worked with Adam before; there was seldom much to laugh about in his programmes.

"At least since it's going out live," Russell murmured, "we'll be spared the endless repetitions when someone fluffs a line. Believe me, it gets progressively harder to laugh at a 'spontaneous' joke you've heard x times before."

At exactly nine thirty the familiar music started up and the opening titles began to roll on the monitors. Gregory Page, the presenter, came down a flight of steps and took his allotted place to dutiful applause.

"Well, ladies and gentlemen," he began, "I wonder how many people would like to be in my shoes tonight?" There was a ripple of laughter.

"There must be any number who have writhed and squirmed under Adam Greenwood's merciless interrogation and wished themselves a thousand miles away. So if anyone in the studio audience has been harbouring a desire to quiz the inquisitor, you'll have your chance at the end of the show.

"Tonight, however, will be a rather different format. We'll be hearing about Adam's memories of growing up here in Shillingham, and also getting a taste of the programmes he'll be hosting over the next five weeks, to celebrate the town's five-hundredth anniversary. So, ladies and gentlemen, please welcome the man himself – Inquisitor Extraordinaire, Adam Greenwood!"

There was a burst of applause and Adam appeared, walking down the steps in his turn and looking, Verity had to admit, extremely handsome in a white dinner jacket which complemented his dark colouring. She reached out to give Eva's hand a reassuring squeeze.

As the interview progressed, both women began to relax. Page showed no sign of trying to needle his guest, deftly leading him into his reminiscences and comparisons of the Shillingham of his boyhood with the town as it was today.

Adam, appearing totally at ease, told some amusing stories about people he had met and the numerous escapades of his schooldays, and, Verity thought, relieved, seemed to be carrying the audience along with him.

Under Page's prompting, he then moved on to outline the venues he'd be using over the next few weeks, and the proposed content of each programme. The first one would come from the Arts Complex – new since his day and in the vanguard of modern thinking, combining, as it did, theatre, library, art gallery and concert hall under one roof. Their subject on that occasion would be the evolvement of the arts over five centuries, with contributions from the historian Mary Derringer and Sir Julian Harwood, resident conductor of the Shillingham Philharmonic Orchestra.

The following week, at Ashbourne School for Girls, the evolvement of education would be considered; at the premises of Randal Tovey, the influence of fashion through the ages; at the Town Hall the growth of local government, and so on, but all with a predominantly local bias.

"You've mentioned four venues," Page remarked. "What's the fifth?"

"Danefield the silversmiths," Adam replied. "As you probably know, they've been in the town for hundreds of years and, interestingly enough, were among the first in England to produce Apostle spoons."

"Really? When would that have been, then?"

"Towards the end of the fifteenth century. Which means they span the whole of our five-hundred-year period."

"Thus rounding things off very neatly. You've jogged my memory, though; by 'Apostle spoons', you mean the ones with the figure of a saint on the handle? I'd forgotten all about them, but my gran had a set."

"So did my parents. As a child, I was fascinated by the little figures, and the fact that they could be identified by what they're carrying. In fact, they still intrigue me, and I'm in the process of building up a collection for myself."

Page looked puzzled. "Can't you just go out and buy them?"

Adam shook his head. "I don't mean teaspoons, it's the original ones I'm after – old, silver spoons about seven inches long. It's an expensive hobby, though – you can pay up to twenty thousand pounds for a really good one." He smiled at Page's soundless whistle. "Interestingly enough, a complete set comprises thirteen, twelve plus a Master, which is usually Christ."

"That's fascinating – I'd no idea." Page glanced at the floor manager, who was signalling that they were into the last few minutes of the programme. "I'd like to talk a lot more about those Apostles of yours, but unfortunately time's running on and I promised these good folk the chance to have a go at you."

Adam turned to the audience, raising both hands in mock appeal. "Ladies and gentlemen, I'm at your mercy."

There was some nervous laughter, which tailed off into silence.

"Could we have the house lights up?" Page called, and, as they came on, he scrutinised the sea of faces in front of him. "Well, come on, folks, this is the chance you've all been waiting for! Who's going to start the ball rolling?"

Some brave person at the back put up a hand.

"Yes, sir?"

"I'd like to ask Mr Greenwood whose idea it was to do these programmes?"

Page frowned, clearly disappointed at the mildness of the question, but Adam was answering smoothly, "Actually, it was mine. I still feel I belong to Shillingham, and I wanted to join in the celebrations."

A round of applause.

"Right – anyone else?"

A few more questions followed, each as innocuous as the first. Perhaps, Verity thought, the people of Shillingham were reluctant to attack one of their own; or maybe they were sympathetically aware of his family in the front row. Whatever the reason for their reticence, the programme was wrapped up without a word spoken in anger; which was as it should be, since this series didn't aim to be confrontational.

Adam and Page retired into the wings and the audience began to file out of the theatre. Verity and Eva exchanged a relieved smile. Imogen leant across Russell to speak to them.

"Adam said not to wait for him; there are always autograph hunters hanging round, and he can't get away without signing at least some of them. But we'd love you to come back for a flat-warming drink, if that's all right? It's looking a lot more civilised now."

They murmured agreement, then Russell said, "I suggest you ladies wait at reception while I go and get the car. As they say, 'I might be some time' – everyone will be leaving at once and there'll probably be a jam."

"In that case," Verity said, "I'll take the opportunity of going to the cloakroom."

She followed the directions she'd been given, down one corridor and into another – what a maze this place was. It was already nearly half-past ten; she hoped Adam wouldn't be delayed too long, and that the drinks session would be brief. She wasn't good at late nights nowadays, and she'd had a busy day.

26

It had been agreed that she'd rejoin the others in the foyer, where they were waiting for Russell. Coming out of the cloakroom, Verity turned right and then left, retracing the way she had come before realising that of course this would lead her back to the studio, not the front hall.

She stopped and looked about her. The corridor stretched blankly in front and behind, lined with closed doors. A few yards ahead it was bisected by another one – which, with luck, might lead in the right direction. She hurried forward, and, as she reached the junction, was in time to see Adam emerge from a door halfway along.

Verity breathed a sigh of relief; he'd be able to direct her. But as she started towards him, an elderly man, who had apparently been waiting for him, caught at his arm and started to speak.

Not wanting to intrude, Verity hesitated, her interest quickening when she saw Adam stiffen, then shake his head. The man leant towards him, talking earnestly but too quietly for her to catch the words. Then, as she watched, Adam suddenly shook off the hand still resting on his arm, said something in a low, angry voice, and, turning on his heel, strode off in the opposite direction.

Hastily, Verity retreated round the corner again, and was innocently searching in her bag a few feet away when the elderly man, clearly distressed, passed the junction without glancing in her direction.

She snapped her handbag shut and started after him. Adam would not, after all, be any use to her, but perhaps this gentleman was making for the exit.

Much to her relief this proved to be the case, and as she joined her party, her guide disappeared through the doors into the night. A moment later Louise said, "Here's Russell now," and they followed her out to the waiting car.

There was no sign of Mia when they reached the flat just before eleven, though music could be heard coming from her bedroom.

27

Verity wondered fleetingly if Adam was disappointed that his stepdaughter had not joined the party. The atmosphere between them had seemed somewhat strained over dinner the other evening.

The sitting room, she thought, looking about her, was much the same size as hers and Eva's, though squarer in shape. Some of the furniture had a temporary look about it – a card table in an alcove with three plain chairs round it, a leather stool of the wrong colour providing extra seating. But there were pictures on the wall and an enormous bunch of spring flowers in a vase, and the general impression was decidedly stylish. Verity remembered that Imogen had worked at French Furnishings in East Parade before marrying Adam. For the first time, she wondered what she did now; small and thin, Imogen struck her as a bundle of nervous energy who would not be happy unless fully occupied.

Drinks were poured and they seated themselves around the room, admiring the lighting effects and the colour scheme – caramel and powder-blue. Verity held back a yawn, hoping Adam would not be long, and her mind replayed the curious little scene she'd unintentionally witnessed. Who was that man, and what had passed between him and Adam? He certainly hadn't looked like an autograph hunter. Still, it was none of her business.

As though she had conjured him up, the sound of the front door reached them and Adam himself came into the room. Verity studied him covertly, wondering if the encounter had upset him. She decided that it had; a nerve was jumping in his cheek, and the smiling urbanity they'd seen on stage had disappeared.

"Well," he demanded almost curtly, "How did it go?"

There was a chorus of approval, and Imogen stretched up to kiss his cheek. "You were wonderful, darling – really relaxed and approachable. Keep that up, and you'll have your critics eating out of your hand!"

"God forbid!" He turned away from her. "I thought we were having champagne?"

Imogen flushed. "I was waiting for you." She produced fresh

glasses, the champagne was poured, and Verity discreetly disposed of her gin and tonic behind a pot plant. If she finished that *and* the champagne, she'd never make the stairs up to bed.

Adam, possibly having caught his mother's raised eyebrows, made a visible effort. "A toast, then: to Greenwood and the Greenwoods – not forgetting the Ryders," he added, with a little bow in Verity's direction. "May our shadows never grow less!"

They raised their glasses, and Russell added whimsically, "God bless us, every one!"

Amen to that, Verity added silently, and gave a sudden shiver, as though someone had walked over her grave. Pushing the phrase hastily away, she took a longer drink of champagne. All would be well. Of course it would.

Three

"I thought Adam seemed a bit off last night," Louise remarked from the top of a ladder, as she positioned little-used volumes on the highest shelf of the bookcase. "Back at the flat, I mean. He nearly bit poor Imogen's head off."

"Well, you know Adam," Russell said philosophically. "Mercurial as always. Perhaps the autograph hunters hassled him."

"He'd got off lightly enough earlier, with everyone bending over backwards to avoid annoying him."

"Nonsense; the purpose of the programme was to preview the next five, so there was no room for controversy. There wasn't expected to be."

"Didn't you think something was wrong, though, later?" Louise persisted, coming down the ladder. "I definitely got the impression he couldn't wait to be rid of us. We didn't even get top-ups of champagne."

"Ah, so that's what's peeving you!"

She threw him a resigned look. "Have it your own way; he was his usual sunny self."

"Seriously, darling, you know he's always edgy after a programme, convinced he could have handled questions better and so on. I'm sure that's all it was."

"After such a smooth performance as last night?"

Russell shrugged. "Anyway, to change the subject, I was thinking about Sunday lunch: shall we invite *les mères*?"

"Elliott and Maggie will be here, had you forgotten? I don't know how long they'll be staying – they mightn't have time for a

31

sit-down meal, but we'll have to make the gesture. And if we ask *them*, we'll have to invite Adam, Imogen and Mia, which would bring the numbers to eleven."

Russell groaned. "So much for leading separate existences!"

"Well, this is exceptional; the flats won't normally be occupied."

"So what do we do?"

"Ring Elliott and ask what his plans are. If he's on for lunch, we'll invite the others; if not, just Mother and Eva."

"You're a gem," Russell said, putting an arm round her.

"That's why you married me," she said.

It was only when the doorbell rang for the second time that Mia remembered she was alone in the flat, and reluctantly slid off her bed to go and answer it. She was taken aback to find Tom Greenwood on the step.

"Hi!" he greeted her.

"Hi."

"Are you busy?"

"What, now?" He nodded. "No, I was just reading."

"Like to come ten-pin bowling? Or squash, if you'd rather? I hear they've got all kinds of facilities at the sports centre."

As she hesitated, he gave her an engaging grin. "Or, if you're not the sporty type, we could go to the cinema."

She smiled back, coming to a sudden decision. "Ten-pin would be fine. You'd better come in while I write a note for Mum. They're both out."

He followed her into the sunny kitchen, waiting as she located pad and pencil.

"Did you go along to the studios last night?" he asked. She shook her head, her hair screening her face as she wrote. "Watch it on TV?"

"No."

Tom said quietly, "It must be tough, having someone else thrust on you. Instead of your real father, I mean."

Mia looked up, surprised at his understanding. "Yes."

"Uncle Adam's not the easiest of people, but his bark's worse than his bite, you know."

"The trouble is, he does an awful lot of barking!"

Tom laughed. "You just have to roll with it. That's what my cousins do."

She looked at him quickly, never having spared much thought for Adam's children. "It can't be easy for them, either."

"Nope. When parents screw up like that, it's not only their own lives they mess up."

Mia propped the note against the toaster, took the door key off a hook and slipped it into her pocket. It was spring, the sun was shining, and it seemed she had a new friend. For the first time in a long while, she felt carefree and happy.

"OK," she said, "I'm ready. Let's go."

This was the way they'd come last night, Verity realised, as, following Naomi's directions, she approached the Marlton road. Presumably she'd turn off before the studios, though, because the instructions didn't mention such an obvious landmark.

'Pass the grammar school on your right and the high school on your left,' she read, 'then take the second right-hand turn.'

And here she was. Rankin Road was composed of fairly large houses built between the wars, several of which had now been turned into flats. Naomi's was number twenty-three, some two-thirds of the way along and directly opposite a small cul-de-sac.

The house had the usual thirties features of gables and bay windows, and was pebbledashed in a dirty cream. There was a full-size window in the gable and a skylight farther along, which would no doubt be Naomi's studio. The front garden was concreted over and two cars were parked there, a black Golf and a blue Renault which Verity recognised as her daughter's. Better to leave her own car in the road, she decided.

Three bells were ranged alongside the front door, Naomi's being the top one. Verity pressed it and waited. After a minute there was the sound of running feet on the stairs, the door was flung open, and she was folded into an enthusiastic embrace. Then Naomi held her at arm's length, smilingly studying her face.

"How *are* you, Mother? The move hasn't been too much of a strain?"

"Not really. I hated leaving Oxford, of course, but once I'd dried my eyes and set off, it was all rather exciting. Oh, and thank you so much for the gorgeous flowers, darling. They immediately made me feel at home."

"That's what I hoped," Naomi said, tucking her arm through Verity's and drawing her into the hall. "It's one of my earliest memories – wherever we lived, the house was always full of flowers.

"I'm afraid we haven't a lift," she added, steering Verity up the stairs, "and what's more there are two flights, since I have what is euphemistically called 'the studio flat'."

"What's euphemistic about it?" Verity objected. "You sculpt up there, after all."

"True, and I do have a north light, though that would be more important if I were painting. What I mean is, the rooms aren't extra large or anything. Funny to think you haven't seen it when I've been here eighteen months, but it seemed easier for me to come to you, and anyway I loved going home."

She paused. "Sorry, that was tactless. Now, are you ready for the next flight or would you like a breather?"

"Of course not – I'm not in my dotage yet!"

There was a door at the top of the staircase which was standing open. Naomi closed it behind them, and Verity found herself on a larger landing that she'd anticipated.

"Yes, it's really quite spacious," Naomi commented, seeing her surprise. "The conversion was very well done, making use of all the roof space as well as the three original attics. Consequently I have four quite decent-sized rooms, plus shower and loo, and a nice modern little kitchen."

She opened each door in turn for her mother's inspection, revealing a pleasant sitting room, two bedrooms, the smaller of which had a man's towelling robe behind the door, and the room with the skylight, which, as Verity had surmised, was the studio. A piece of work, covered with a towel, stood on a table.

"May I see?" Verity asked, nodding towards it.

"Of course. I only finished it yesterday." She lifted the cloth, and Verity found herself looking at a handsome, somewhat austere face that she recognised.

"Sir Julian Harwood!" she exclaimed. "It's a wonderful likeness, dear – how clever you are."

"I am quite pleased with it. The Arts Complex commissioned it for the quincentennial; it will stand in the entrance to the concert hall, and Sir Julian will be unveiling it. I'm not sure of the date yet, but I'll make sure you and Lou have tickets.

"Well, that's the end of the tour, so let's sit down and have a sherry and you can tell me all the news."

"You've more space than you had before, haven't you?" Verity commented as they went into the sitting room.

"Oh, yes, and apart from that, this location's so much better. I was out in the sticks at Frecklemarsh, whereas here I can walk almost everywhere. The far end of Rankin Road leads to the High Street, which is wonderfully convenient."

Verity nodded, accepting the sherry. The difference between her daughters never failed to amaze her; Louise, like Verity herself, enjoyed having pretty things about her, whereas Naomi had never cared for possessions, living happily for years in what her parents had regarded as a garret and indignantly refusing all their tactful offers of help.

And she could look so lovely, Verity thought wistfully, if only she'd do something with herself. As it was, with her cotton skirt swishing about her ankles and her hair hanging straight and unadorned, she looked more like a student than a woman of forty-five. If only she'd meet someone suitable and settle down.

35

"Now –" Naomi curled up in an easy chair – "tell me about the maisonette. Are you sure you've done the right thing?"

"Oh, definitely," Verity answered and realised, as she spoke, that her last reservations had gone. "I have a most attractive bedsitter, and there's a very pleasant room downstairs where Eva and I have supper, discuss the day's news and watch television. And of course it's lovely to have both you and Louise so near, after all these years. I'm longing to show you everything; *you* must come and lunch with *me*."

"I'd love to." Naomi sipped her drink. "I saw Adam on the box last night."

"Ah yes; we all went along to the studio."

"Quite the pussy cat, wasn't he? I kept waiting for a snarl but none came."

Not until they reached home, Verity thought.

"My protégé, for want of a better word, was most intrigued to learn I know the famous Greenwoods."

"And where is your protégé?"

"Dispatched for the day – I wanted you to myself. How's Russell? Any more trips planned?"

Obviously she'd no intention of discussing the owner of the dressing-gown. "Yes indeed," Verity replied, "he's off to Peru in a month or so. I'm green with envy – it's somewhere I've always wanted to go – but I suppose I'll have to be content with viewing it second-hand."

"And Lou? I haven't seen her for a while. In her element, I expect, putting her new nest in order." Which was so close to what Verity herself had been thinking that, caught off-balance, she did not reply.

"She phoned earlier," Naomi was continuing, "to invite me for Sunday lunch. Apparently there'll be quite a crowd of you, but unfortunately I can't make it. All the same, it looks as though I'll be doing well for free meals now my relatives have moved in. And talking of meals, I'd better see to lunch. It's only salad, I hope that's all right."

It was, in fact, what Verity had expected. Naomi looked on cooking as an unnecessary time-waster, but she was at least skilful with salads and had devised some original and appetising ones. Verity doubted if she ate much else.

Today's was served with a crisp white wine and followed by fruit and cheese, all partaken of on trays balanced on their knees. Verity thought briefly of Louise's elegant table settings, and hid a smile. As long as both her girls were happy, *vive la différence*.

They sat for some time over coffee, talking of family and mutual friends, and it was nearly four o'clock when Verity rose to go.

"It's been lovely, darling, thank you so much. I'll give you a ring after the weekend and fix a return visit."

Naomi walked downstairs with her and saw her out. "I should turn in the gateway if I were you," she suggested, "and go back the way you came. The High Street gets very congested, specially on Friday afternoons."

Verity took her advice and was grateful to find the Marlton road relatively quiet – though once the schools went back, things would be different.

A couple of hundred yards along were some traffic lights which, annoyingly, turned red as she approached. She wound down the window, idly scanning the pedestrians on the opposite pavement as she did so; young mothers with prams, businessmen hurrying to appointments, older women with shopping baskets.

And it was then that she saw him, the man from the studio who'd tried to speak to Adam. Small and grey, he was standing in the middle of the pavement and creating something of a log-jam as passers-by from both directions manoeuvred their way past him.

As she watched he seemed to realise this, because she saw him give an apologetic little smile before, in a belated attempt to make way, he stepped out on to the road just as the lights changed.

What happened next took place with the speed of light, but for ever afterwards replayed itself in her head in slow motion, like dreams when, with weighted legs, it's impossible to move however urgent the need.

There was no traffic drawn up on the other side of the lights, but a car which had been approaching slowly preparatory to stopping accelerated as they changed, and though the driver braked violently, there was not time to stop before colliding with the pedestrian, who, seeing it too late, stood frozen like a rabbit in headlights.

Gasping with horror, Verity wrenched open the door and, regardless of the queue of traffic which had formed behind her, ran across the road to the limp figure. The force of impact had hurled him back towards the pavement, and he was lying with his head on the kerb. An ominous trickle of blood was beginning to flow from it.

Verity knelt beside him, feeling feverishly for his pulse. It was a mere flutter, weak and erratic.

"Someone phone an ambulance," she said urgently over her shoulder, "and hurry!"

The man's eyes flickered open. "How careless of me," he murmured. "I'm – so sorry."

"You're all right," she lied. "Try not to move, help is on the way." She looked up at the circle of shocked faces above her. "Someone has—?"

"Yes, they're phoning now."

Verity took off her jacket and draped it over the prone figure. Only then, as she started to loosen the clothing round his neck, did she see that he was wearing a clerical collar.

She was easing it from his throat when, to her startled surprise, he reached up and caught hold of her hand. His eyes were open again, fixed on hers with a desperation impossible to ignore.

"It's all right," Verity repeated soothingly, "someone—"

He made a slight, impatient movement of his head, and she saw he was again trying to speak, though this time it seemed more of an effort. The white lips opened and closed several times

38

as Verity stroked his hand, hoping to impart reassurance. Then the words came – breathless, barely audible, and she bent closer to hear them.

"The – Twelve – Apostles," he said.

Verity looked at him blankly. His eyes were pleading with her, begging her to understand. "The Twelve Apostles?" she repeated.

His head moved in a faint nod as though satisfied. "Ask—" he whispered. But the effort had exhausted him, and his eyes closed. To Verity's unutterable relief, the sound of an ambulance siren was growing steadily louder.

It was only when practised hands took over from her and someone gently helped her to her feet that she became aware of sounds that had been in the background all along – a desperate sobbing and repeated murmurs of "No, oh please no!" She turned to see a young woman, pale and shaking, her hands pressed to her mouth, and realised she must be the driver who had hit him.

Her own role, such as it was, having been taken over, reaction set in and Verity herself started shaking, gratefully reclaiming her jacket as one of the paramedics handed it to her.

The next few minutes passed in a blur. A shop-keeper brought out two wooden chairs and she and the driver were seated on them and given glasses of water. Blue-uniformed figures had materialised and some were interviewing the crowd, now thinning, while others set up roadblocks and redirected the traffic. Verity's own car, at the head of the queue by the lights, still had its offside door open. Vaguely, she wished someone would close it.

There was a diversion when a woman came pushing through the crowd just as the stretcher was lifted and put into the ambulance. "It's not the Reverend, is it?" she gasped. "Someone said – oh, my dear Lor', it is!"

"You know this gentleman, madam?" A policeman was instantly at her side.

"Yes—" She was following the actions of the paramedics, watching as the ambulance doors were shut and the vehicle, siren starting up again, began to move away.

The woman turned her anxious face back to the constable. "It's the Reverend Morrison. He stayed with us last night. Is he hurt bad?"

"Us?" queried the policeman.

"I work at the Tivoli – you know, up the road."

"The Tivoli Hotel?"

"That's right. He arrived lateish – phoned ahead to book a room, so we knew he was coming, like. But he checked out today about eleven, said he was getting the midday train back to London."

So he'd come for just the one night, thought Verity, who couldn't help overhearing. Surely not for the sole purpose of attending Adam's programme? If he lived in London, there'd have been plenty of chances to do so there. And if he'd intended catching the midday train, what was he doing here at four fifteen?

"Are you all right?" asked a voice closer at hand. It was the policewoman who had helped her to the chair.

"I shall be, in a minute or two." Verity looked up into the young woman's concerned face.

"Take your time, there's no hurry. My name's Patsy Vane, and you are . . .?"

"Verity Ryder," answered Verity through dry lips.

"Did you know the gentleman involved, Mrs Ryder?"

"No, but I—" Verity broke off and shook her head, not having the strength to embark on a lengthy explanation. The hotel would supply his name and address; what did it matter if she'd caught sight of him last night? It wouldn't alter anything.

"I take it you witnessed the accident?" PC Vane was continuing. "Are you able to tell me what happened?"

"I'd stopped at the lights," Verity said unsteadily, "and I saw him standing in the middle of the pavement." She looked up suddenly, remembering. "He had a briefcase; did . . .?"

"Yes, it's gone with him in the ambulance."

Verity nodded. "Then suddenly, just as the lights changed, he stepped out into the road." She glanced along the pavement to where the still-sobbing young woman was also being interviewed. "It really wasn't the driver's fault."

"But if the vehicle had been stationary at the lights, how did it get up enough speed to—?"

Verity was shaking her head. "It wasn't stationary, it was coming along towards us, slowing down ready to stop. When the lights changed, it accelerated. And . . ." She gave a helpless little shrug.

Seeing her distress, the policewoman didn't question her further except to ask for her address, after which Verity was driven home in her own car, with a police vehicle following behind. The Marlton road was abnormally deserted, a fact explained when they reached King Street by a large diversion board blocking entry. Minutes later, to Verity's untold relief, they were drawing up outside the electronic gates of Greenwood. She reached for the operating button, and they swung open.

"Most impressive!" murmured Patsy Vane, driving through while the police car waited outside. "Shall I garage it for you?"

"No, don't worry." Helpful though she'd been, Verity suddenly needed to be rid of her and all her associations. "My daughter will do it later," she added.

"Very well. There is somebody at home?"

"Oh yes, yes, thank you."

"All right, Mrs Ryder. Well, take it easy, you've had a nasty shock. A colleague and I'll come round in the morning, if that's all right, and take a formal statement."

Verity watched her walk back through the gates just as they were closing, climb into the police car, and be driven away.

"Mother? Was that the police?"

Verity turned as Louise and Russell came hurrying out of their front door.

"Are you all right? Oh God, nothing's happened to Naomi?"

"Naomi," Verity said distinctly, "is fine. But I – need to sit down."

She felt herself sway, was aware of Louise's startled exclamation and Russell's supporting arm as he half-carried her into the house and settled her in an easy chair. A moment later a glass of brandy was put in her hand and she sipped it gratefully, before looking up at their anxious faces.

"Could you ask Eva to come? I don't want to go through this twice."

"Of course." Russell went to buzz her on the intercom.

Verity took another sip of brandy and said carefully, "Is Adam around?"

Louise looked surprised. "No, they're all out, including Mia," she smiled, "who's gone ten-pin bowling with Tom. But what do you want with Adam?"

Verity shook her head. "It doesn't matter."

Eva came hurrying in, her anxious eyes going from Verity to the brandy. "What is it, V? What's happened?"

Verity drew a deep breath and put down the glass. "On the way home from Naomi's just now, I – witnessed a road accident. An elderly gentleman was knocked down."

They all exclaimed together, regarding her with consternation.

"I'd stopped at the lights," Verity went on, willing her voice to remain steady, "so I saw everything. He – was standing on the pavement –" she felt she would be repeating this in her sleep – "and he suddenly stepped off into the road, just as the lights changed. The driver hadn't a chance."

"What did you do?"

"Well, I rushed over to him, of course, to see if I could help. He'd hit his head on the kerb and it was bleeding. He – didn't look too good." She paused, remembering. "I felt his pulse, which was very faint, and tried to loosen his collar, which wasn't easy because he was a clergyman." She caught her breath. "Still is, I hope."

"Go on." Russell's calm tone steadied her.

42

"I put my jacket over him for extra warmth, and then I just – held his hand till the ambulance arrived."

"Was he conscious?"

"At first. He actually apologised for causing the accident." Verity choked to a halt. She'd intended telling them what else he'd said, but was unable to continue and, to spare her, the others took over, talking to her gently, calming her, and the moment passed.

But she needed to tell someone, and after supper a few hours later, she said abruptly, "I'd seen him before, Eva."

"The man who was knocked down?"

"Yes; he was at the studio last night."

Eva stared at her. "At hospitality, you mean?"

"No – at least, if he was, I didn't notice him. But on my way back from the cloakroom I saw him talking to Adam."

"Adam? But – I don't understand. Why didn't you say so before?"

"I was going to, but . . ." Verity shrugged. "And that's not all. Just before he lost consciousness, he gripped my hand and said: 'The Twelve Apostles.' "

"He said *what*?"

"I know – it sounds mad, doesn't it, but whatever he meant, it was desperately important to him."

"I think Adam should hear this," Eva said firmly. "I'll give him a buzz."

Verity lay back in her chair and closed her eyes, heard Eva say, "Adam? Can you come straight over? Verity has something to tell you . . . No, I'll explain when you get here."

Minutes later Eva answered his knock and he came frowningly into the room, not pleased at having his evening disturbed. "What's this all about, then?"

Eva glanced at Verity, who remained silent. "V saw someone knocked down on her way back from Naomi's. She went to help him, and – she recognised him."

"I saw him talking to you last night," Verity said flatly.

43

"I talked to a lot of people."

"This was later, after the show. You were in the corridor."

There was a brief silence. Verity met and held Adam's eyes. Then he said lightly, "Must have been an autograph hunter."

"I don't think so. He put a hand on your arm and you shook him off and walked away."

Adam smiled humourlessly. "Definitely an autograph hunter."

"Tell him what he said, V," Eva put in.

Verity moistened her lips. "He tried to speak several times before he managed it. It was obviously very important to him. When the words finally came they were just a whisper, but I heard them quite distinctly. He said, 'The Twelve Apostles.' "

For a long minute nobody spoke. Then Adam said, "Just that?"

"He started to say something else, but only got as far as 'Ask—' before he passed out again."

Adam, who had been leaning forward, sat back in his chair. "Well, you could be right, I suppose; perhaps he *was* there last night, and in his delirium remembered hearing about my spoons."

"He was a clergyman," Eva added.

"Ah! Then he was probably thinking on quite different lines." Adam looked at the clock. "We might just catch the local news; there could be an update on him."

They were only just in time; as he switched on, the announcer was saying, "An elderly man, believed to be a clergyman from Surrey, was knocked down this afternoon on the Marlton road in Shillingham. He died in hospital without regaining consciousness."

Verity's hand went to her mouth. It was Eva who switched off the set as the weather forecast began.

Adam got to his feet. "Too bad the Florence Nightingale act didn't work," he said briskly. "Never mind, he'll be with his Twelve Apostles now, and can sort them out for himself."

"Adam!" Eva was outraged.

He lifted an eyebrow. "Of course I'm sorry the old boy's dead – can't afford to lose any fans, after all – but really, Ma, I haven't a clue who he was, so I can't help. Now, if you'll excuse me, Imogen will be wondering what's going on."

And with a brief nod in their direction, he let himself out.

Verity closed her eyes, feeling the slow tears run down her cheeks. What was it about the Twelve Apostles that Mr – Morrison, was it? – had thought it so imperative to pass on to her? She'd never know now, and felt miserably that she had failed him.

Eva said gently, "It's time you were in bed. You go on up and I'll bring you a hot drink. And, V, don't fret about Adam. You know how it is, he talks for effect – it's his job, after all. He doesn't mean half what he says."

"No," Verity agreed, wearily pulling herself to her feet. But Adam had known very well whom she was speaking about; of that she had no doubt. So why had he pretended otherwise?

Four

V erity was having breakfast when Naomi phoned the next morning.

"Mother – I've just spoken to Louise. I'm so terribly sorry about what happened – and it's all my fault. If I hadn't suggested your avoiding the High Street—"

"Nonsense, dear, it was nobody's fault. These things happen." Verity wished she felt as philosophical as she sounded.

"I believe the man died?"

"I'm afraid so, yes."

"All the same, I'm sure it was a comfort to him, having you there."

He *had* looked more at peace, Verity reflected, when his eyes finally closed: perhaps because he thought she'd promised to do what he wanted.

"The police are coming this morning," she said aloud. "Something about a statement. I'm not sure what more they want – I told them what happened." Or most of it, and she still didn't think the omission either important or relevant. It wasn't, after all, as if Morrison had been killed deliberately.

After she'd put the phone down, she sat for a minute looking out of the window. The table where she breakfasted – still, luxuriously, in her dressing-gown – was in the bay window and gave her a bird's-eye view. From where she sat she could see part of the garden with its gates and the surrounding wall, the hill down to town, now clogged with traffic, and some of the road opposite, where Sir Julian and Lady Harwood lived, and along

47

which a postman was now cycling. It was another sunny day –
but one which the Reverend Mr Morrison wouldn't see.

Had he a wife? Verity wondered, with a shaft of painful
sympathy. And if so, would she know what had brought him
hotfoot to Shillingham?

And why, she wondered, unable to put the man out of her
mind, had he stayed at the Tivoli? It was a shabby hotel with little
to recommend it, yet he'd made a point of booking a room in
advance. Because it was cheap, and he had to watch his finances?
That was quite possible. Or – and Verity felt herself go hot –
because of its proximity to the television studios, which were only
a short bus ride up the road?

She stood up suddenly, rocking the table and spilling some
coffee in her saucer. There was nothing to be gained by all this
speculation; Adam had said categorically that he didn't know the
man, and short of accusing him of lying, she had to leave it there.
Whatever her somewhat ambivalent feelings about him, he was
her godson and the son of her dearest friend; the last thing she
wanted was to cause him any trouble.

Automatically she started to clear the table. After she'd seen
the police this morning, she resolved, she would put the whole
thing out of her mind and concentrate on settling into her new
life here at Greenwood.

While Verity was reaching this decision, Eva, newspaper
propped unread on the breakfast bar, was pursuing her own
uneasy thoughts.

Adam knew something about that man, she was sure of it.
At first she'd wondered if it was a case of mistaken identity on
V's part; from what she'd said, they'd been some distance from
her at the studio, and one elderly man looked much like
another. It was her son's attitude that had convinced her
otherwise. Something was clearly troubling him, and it could
well be that this clergyman, whom he had denied meeting, was
at the root of it.

Oh God, Eva thought, on an unaccustomed wave of help-lessness, I wish Max was here!

Scott Perry stood in the doorway watching his wife feed their baby. They looked, he thought almost reverently, like an Old Master painting – Judy's bent head, the fall of her hair as she gazed down on her first-born, the baby's starlike hand on her breast. Even the blue throw over the wicker nursing-chair en-hanced the impression.

But hard on the fancy came an unwelcome picture of Imogen with Mia at much the same age. He'd felt the same protective love then as he felt for his present wife and child; might this tenderness also end in recriminations and tears? He had a frightening vision of himself in, say, fifteen years' time, another broken marriage behind him, embittered and alone.

He turned abruptly from the doorway, unwilling to disturb the calm of mother and child with his forebodings, and, in turning, caught a glimpse of himself in the hall mirror.

Deliberately he walked over and stood staring at his reflection: a long face with furrowed forehead, deep-set grey eyes – also with lines round them – a thin nose, chin still unshaven. What in God's name did Judy see in him? He was almost old enough to be her father. No wonder poor little Mia felt awkward coming here.

Adam bloody Greenwood! he thought on a wave of bitterness. It was all his fault! That arrogant, conceited son-of-a-bitch had taken first Imogen and then Mia away from him. All right, so he'd managed to build a new life for himself, but no thanks to Greenwood. Someone ought to teach that man a lesson.

Perry thought back to the programme which, at Judy's in-sistence, they had watched the other evening.

"He's very attractive, isn't he?" she'd remarked.

Judy, of all people! Then, realising what she'd said, her hand had flown, childlike, to her mouth as her wide eyes regarded him apprehensively.

"Oh darling, I didn't mean – I only—" and he had covered her hand with his, putting an end to her apology. But she'd *thought* it, that was clear. First Imogen, now Judy, and, looking at the surly face in the mirror, who could blame them?

Judy's reflection appeared behind his own, the sleeping child in her arms, and he turned quickly to face her, uncomfortable at being caught staring at himself.

But all she said was, "What time is Mia coming?"

"For lunch – about twelve, I suppose. You don't mind, do you, love?" he added anxiously.

She threw him an affectionate glance. "Of course I don't mind. She's your daughter, as much as Rosie is."

He watched her walk carefully up the stairs, her legs bare under the short dressing-gown. Then, sighing, he started after her. It was time he showered and shaved.

The police arrived promptly at eleven, Patsy Vane and a solid young man she introduced as PC Kenworthy.

"It's quite simple, Mrs Ryder," she reassured Verity. "Just tell me in your own words what you saw yesterday, and PC Kenworthy will take it down verbatim. I might need to interrupt you if something isn't clear or we need more details. Then, when you've finished, we'll ask you to read the statement through, make any corrections you might think necessary and initial them, then sign it. We'll also ask you to sign an endorsement confirming that what you've said is a true account and that you realise it might be given in evidence."

Verity frowned. "Evidence of what?"

"Basically the cause of death, in this instance. As a witness, your testimony will be crucial in determining the verdict at the inquest – whether it was death by misadventure or unlawful killing."

"Inquest?" Verity's heartbeats quickened.

"Yes, you'll be required to attend the Coroner's Court in Carrington Street at ten o'clock on Monday."

Verity swallowed, her mouth dry. "I thought this statement was the end of my involvement."

"Unfortunately not."

"But I – you're surely not saying the driver's fate depends on what I remember?"

"Not entirely, no. We have other witnesses, and of course the skid marks have been measured to check the speed at which the vehicle was travelling."

"She didn't have a chance," Verity said firmly. "He just stepped out, without looking to left or right."

"Perhaps he'd something on his mind," mused PC Vane. But Verity preferred not to speculate on that.

So yet again she was led through her account, and with each repetition the gruesome scenes conjured up were etched more deeply on her memory.

"Did he speak at all?" Patsy Vane enquired, when she came to the end.

Verity threw her a startled glance. "He said he was sorry," she replied after a minute. "For the accident, I suppose." Another hesitation. "And he did murmur something later, but it was hard to make out."

True enough, though she'd managed it. That sin of omission was for you, Eva. But suppose, Verity thought in panic, someone else at the scene had heard, if not Morrison's dying words, her own repetition of them? She would just have to say she was confused, that she'd forgotten.

Only half-concentrating, she read through the handwritten statement. No alterations were necessary. She signed it together with the endorsement and the police officers stood up to go.

"Will you be able to make your own way to Carrington Street, or . . .?"

"Oh yes, thank you. My friend or one of my daughters will come with me." She opened the front door for them. "Was he married, Mr Morrison?"

"Widowed, I believe. At any rate, it's his daughter and son-in-law who'll attend the inquest."

51

As Verity closed the door, Eva came down the stairs. "How did it go?"

"Somewhat unnerving." She met her friend's eye and answered her unspoken question. "No, I didn't mention either Adam or the Twelve Apostles."

Eva gave her a quick hug. "Bless you. I'm sure they're not relevant anyway. Now, to turn to more pleasant things, has Louise mentioned Sunday lunch? I hear it's to be *en famille* – including Elliott and Maggie, who'll be down." She smiled. "A superabundance of Greenwoods, I fear."

But Verity's mind was still on the clergyman. "Eva, I have to attend the inquest on Monday. Will you come with me? Louise and Naomi will offer, I'm sure, but they don't know all the facts and it's just possible something might come up."

Eva looked alarmed. "About Adam, you mean?"

"If Mr Morrison came specifically to see him."

"You think he did?"

"Eva, I don't *know*!"

"You poor love," Eva said after a minute. "What a ghastly time you're having, and Adam's at least partly to blame. Of course I'll come; quite apart from lending moral support, I need to hear everything for myself."

She squeezed Verity's arm. "In the meantime, though, let's try to put it out of our minds and enjoy the weekend. I was wondering if we should get some terracotta pots for the terrace? Shall we go to the garden centre and have a look round?"

And Verity, accepting that nothing she could do would alter Monday's proceedings, nodded her agreement.

By lunchtime, Imogen had completed all that needed to be done in the flat, and the afternoon stretched emptily ahead. She was alone; Adam was spending the day with his children and wouldn't be home till late, and Mia was at Scott and Judy's.

Though not by choice, Imogen recalled. Young Tom had asked her out again, and she'd clearly rather have gone with him. Their friendship had taken Imogen by surprise. Her daughter had previously shown no interest in boys – or perhaps vice versa – but Tom seemed a nice lad, and good-looking, too, like all the Greenwoods, with his father's dark, curly hair.

Imogen wished she felt more at home with her husband's family; Elliott, who lived in London, was the one they saw most of, but she didn't enjoy his company, finding him immature and full of his own importance. He and Maggie seemed to be acting all the time – and perhaps they were. At any rate, she didn't know where she was with them. Come to that, life with Adam could also be unpredictable.

She frowned, standing at the patio window and staring down the garden. He'd been looking forward to the six weeks here in Shillingham, but something was worrying him. For the last two nights he'd been extremely restless, interrupting her own sleep with his tossing and turning.

It had started the night of the transmission, though at first she hadn't noticed. Adam was always on a high after a broadcast, manifested either by displays of irritability or wild exuberance – the residue, she assumed, of the nervous energy he'd called on for his performance and the last of which was channelled into their lovemaking, which invariably took place after a broadcast.

On Thursday, therefore, when he had snapped at her – embarrassingly in front of the family – it had come as no surprise. But his lovemaking that night had had a frenzied edge to it which was new and disquieting, and at the end of it, instead of falling asleep as he usually did, he'd held her tightly against him, his face buried in her hair.

"We have a good life, don't we, Imogen?" he'd said, adding with an undercurrent of urgency, "You do love me?"

It was so unlike Adam to need reassurance of any kind that she'd been alarmed.

"Of course I love you! Darling, what is it? Is something wrong?"

Whereupon he had released her with a long, shuddering sigh. "No," he'd replied, adding enigmatically, "I shan't let there be."

And added to all that was the strange summons from Eva last night. When Adam had returned some ten minutes later, he'd walked straight to the drinks table and poured himself a stiff whisky.

"What was all that about?" Imogen had asked curiously.

"God knows. Some cock-and-bull story about Verity seeing an old boy knocked down by a car. I can't imagine what they expected me to do about it."

Imogen, puzzled, had sensed this was not the full explanation. It was, though, apparently all he was going to tell her.

Now, disconsolately, she turned from the window. She should get some lunch, but she was tired of her own company and the thought of sitting by herself at the little makeshift card table did not appeal.

Christina! she thought suddenly on a wave of inspiration. She'd phone and see if she were free. It was a measure of how busy she'd been over the last few days that she'd not yet contacted the woman with whom she used to work and who'd been one of her closest friends.

Saturdays were busy at French Furnishings, Imogen recalled, dialling the shop rather than her friend's home number. And sure enough she was put through and Christina was exclaiming with pleasure and assuring her that of course she was free for lunch. They arranged to meet in half an hour at the Vine Leaf, the wine bar where they'd often lunched in the past.

Her mood suddenly lightened, Imogen was hurriedly changing when the phone rang, and she lifted it to hear her daughter's voice.

"Just letting you know I'll be late home," Mia told her. "Daddy's taking me to the cinema."

"Fine. I'll expect you when I see you, then." And, catching up her handbag, Imogen went out to the car.

"If she hadn't gone poking her nose in," Nigel remarked offhandedly in reference to Verity, "she wouldn't be in this fix."

"Poking her nose in?" Naomi repeated. "Is that what you call going to someone's assistance?"

He shrugged. "Other people were around – someone would have helped him. It wasn't as if she'd knocked him down herself. Fancied playing the Good Samaritan, I dare say, and look where it's got her. All I'm saying is, it serves her right for interfering."

Naomi drew a deep breath, metaphorically counting to ten. This ridiculous conversation was the result of her comment that she was going to phone her mother to ask how the police interview had gone.

Nigel, unaware – or at least dismissive – of her anger, bit noisily into the apple he was eating and the juice spurted on to his chin. Naomi regarded him disparagingly. How had she ever thought he had talent? To her knowledge, he'd not written a line in the six months he'd been under her roof, and she'd discovered he was not above helping himself to the odd fiver if she left her purse lying around.

But this needling animosity, now always present, dated from his discovery of her friendship with the Greenwoods. Why this should be so she'd no idea, unless it was underlying resentment, envy of people he regarded as more fortunate than himself.

"Anybody could do what he does!" he'd remarked of Adam when the programme ended. "Born with one of his silver spoons in his mouth, that's all. These people really bug me – think they're better than the rest of us, poncing around on TV. Twenty thousand for one lousy spoon! God, what I could do with half that amount!"

He'd even had the gall to suggest she persuade Elliott to recite some of his poetry in public. "All I need is a break," he'd cajoled, the whine in his voice setting her teeth on edge. "If Elliott High-and-Mighty Greenwood read it, the critics would sit up and take notice and my name would be made."

"So although you despise him and his family," she had said coldly, "you're quite prepared to make use of him?"

"He'd do it if you asked him – lifelong friend, and all that."

55

"We'll never know," Naomi replied, "since I've no intention of doing so."

At which Nigel had lost his temper. "You don't really want me to succeed, do you?" he'd flung at her. "You'd rather keep me here as a lapdog, licking your boots and ready to jump into bed whenever the fancy takes you!"

Her reaction was instinctive, a stinging slap across his face before she'd time to consider the wisdom of such an action. For a moment they'd stood unmoving, staring at each other, and she was sure he was going to hit her. Then, greatly to her relief, he'd forced a laugh, said, "Too near the bone, eh?" and slammed out of the flat. They hadn't referred to the incident since.

Today, however, his spite was turned on her mother, whom he'd never even met. Because, yesterday, he'd had to vacate the flat on her account? Whatever, Naomi told herself that she couldn't put up with him any longer. It would be wiser, though, not to give him notice while battle was enjoined, as it were. Better to let things simmer down, and when they were both calmer, quietly suggest that he pack his bags.

She stood up, looking down at him as he gnawed round the apple core. "All I can say is, if ever I have an accident I hope to God you're not the only person around." And she went to make her delayed call.

The Vine Leaf and Christina French were both exactly as Imogen remembered them.

"How long are you here for?" Christina was asking.

"Six weeks at the moment, but the flat's permanent and will be there whenever we need it – when we come to see Mia and Adam's children, for instance."

"I saw Adam on the box the other evening," Christina said. "Very smooth."

"By which you mean he didn't tear anyone's reputation to shreds," Imogen translated.

Christina laughed. "Not exactly, but he is rather fierce on screen, isn't he? I hope he's not like that at home!"

Imogen smiled without replying. It had been to Christina that she'd confided the problems leading to the breakdown of her marriage and her initial attraction to Adam; and for the first time in their friendship, she had felt let down by Christina's response. Though sympathetic and ready to listen, she'd advised Imogen to talk things over with Scott and not commit herself till all attempts at reconciliation had been exhausted.

"But I don't *want* a reconciliation!" Imogen remembered exclaiming. "Things have gone beyond that now! I'm in love, Christy!"

It was all very well for her, Imogen thought rebelliously; hers and Edward's was an ideal marriage. In fact in the early days, she and Scott had wondered why the Frenches had bothered to have children, since each seemingly had eyes only for the other. Nevertheless they'd produced two, both dispatched at the earliest opportunity to local boarding schools, and their daughter Stephanie, like Mia, was a pupil at Ashbourne's.

"How's the family?" Imogen asked now, gracefully moving from her affairs to those of her friend.

"Fine, thanks. Edward's Captain of the Golf Club this year, and he's like a dog with two tails. Ned's doing his GCSEs, and no doubt you get news of Stephie from Mia."

"And the shop? Still flourishing?"

"Yes, though as always it's hard to get the right staff. We're very short-handed, and I'm at my wits' end trying to find someone."

"I could help out," Imogen said impulsively.

Christina laid down her fork. "Do you mean that?"

"For as long as I'm here, yes." Though she'd spoken without thinking it through, this now seemed to Imogen an excellent idea. "Mia will be back at school on Wednesday," she continued, "and Adam spends most of his time working on these programmes. Added to which, although my in-laws are next door, I really haven't much in common with them. To be honest, I was wondering how I was going to fill in my time."

"Well, if you're sure, that would be wonderful – just like old times." Christina paused. "What do you do with yourself in London?"

Imogen shrugged. "Voluntary work, mainly. Stewarding at National Trust properties, working in charity shops, that kind of thing. Nothing very inspired."

"Don't you miss full-time work?"

"I suppose I do, now that I think about it. The stumbling block is Adam's timetable; it's so erratic, and I like to be free when he is. Still, if I get back in the swing with you, I might look for something more permanent when I go back."

"You wouldn't like to be thrown in at the deep end, would you?" Christina asked tentatively. "I shall be working late tonight organising some new displays – I've warned Edward not to expect me back to dinner. It would be marvellous if you could lend a hand. It would help to break you in, and we could have supper somewhere afterwards. Or must you be home by a certain time?"

"Actually, no." Imogen felt a stirring of excitement. She had enjoyed her work at French Furnishings and was already looking forward to being back in harness. "Adam will be late home and Mia phoned as I was leaving, to say Scott's taking her to the cinema. I'd love to join you."

Christina raised her glass. "Then here's to our renewed association, even if it is on a temporary basis!"

To Naomi's surprise, there was no sign of Nigel when she returned from her Saturday shop. Usually she found him prone on the sofa watching a sports programme, and she'd intended to raise the subject of his leaving then and there. The sooner the matter was settled, she felt, the better. However, she was later than usual this afternoon, so the programme might have finished. He could even have gone out to buy the meal.

Though normally they ate separately in the evening, Nigel regarding salad as 'rabbit fodder', he had taken it on himself to provide supper on Saturdays, either by bringing home fish and chips or a curry, or by making the cheese pie which was his speciality and surprisingly good.

Consequently she'd not bought anything for this evening, and she was getting hungry. She unpacked the provisions, put them away, and laid the kitchen table. If he didn't come soon, she'd have to scratch something together and start without him.

Damn him! she thought, he could at least have left a note to say he'd be late. But perhaps he'd fallen asleep on his bed? That had been known, after a lunchtime session in the Hare and Hounds. She went on to the landing and knocked firmly on his door.

"Nigel? Are you there? It's supper time!"

There was no reply. She turned the handle and the door swung open, showing the room to be empty – unnaturally so. It took Naomi a second or two to realise that all his possessions had gone – the bathrobe from behind the door, the clutter which usually littered dressing-table and chest.

She stood looking about her, feeling oddly deflated. It seemed she'd been pre-empted; Nigel, too, had had enough, and taken matters into his own hands. Exactly what else he'd taken in those hands she would no doubt discover after a swift inventory of the flat.

Well, she thought, closing the door, she'd have preferred a more formal ending to their association, but the desired result had been achieved. Tomorrow she'd clean out his room, erase any lingering traces of him. And she'd think very carefully before inviting anyone else to occupy it.

It was nearly eleven o'clock when Scott dropped Mia at Greenwood. The duty visit had passed off better than she could have hoped; Rosie had bestowed toothless smiles on her, Judy had been more relaxed than usual, and best of all, she'd had her father to herself for three whole hours.

"Thanks, Daddy," she said as she opened the car door, "that was really cool."

"Glad you enjoyed it, chicken," Scott replied. "So did I." He should have thought of this before, he chided himself. Given his undivided attention, the child had opened up to him as she hadn't done since the family'd split up.

"On your next exeat we'll do it again," he added.

"That'd be brilliant!" She bent over to kiss his cheek and he put an arm round her, pulling her close for a moment.

"I do love you, you know," he said gruffly.

"Me too. Good-night, Daddy."

He watched her go through the small gate alongside the double ones and start across the forecourt before, with a sigh he didn't analyse, he started the engine and drove away.

Only as she approached her front door did Mia notice that although there were lights in the main house, the flat seemed to be in darkness. Surely Mum at least was in? She'd not said she was going out.

Mia fumbled for her key, put it in the lock, and the door opened on to blackness, warm and impenetrable. The next minute, like something from a nightmare, hands reached out to seize her, spinning her round as an arm pinioned her across the chest and a hand clamped over her mouth.

"Not a sound," hissed a whisper in her ear as she struggled furiously, "or you'll regret it, believe me. Now, sweetheart, where are those bloody spoons?"

The hand moved fractionally to allow her to answer. When she didn't – because she couldn't – he shook her roughly. "Come on, we haven't got all night. I've wasted enough time as it is. Show me where they are, and I won't hurt you."

He had started to pull her inside when, like the answer to her prayers, a pair of headlights blossomed at the gates, which promptly swung open.

Before the glare could illuminate him, her assailant thrust Mia aside and disappeared into the darkness round the side of the house. Her legs giving way, she slid down to the ground and huddled against the wall, crying and shaking. The car screeched to a halt, the door flew open and Adam came running towards her.

"Mia – are you all right? My God, what's happened?"

He raised her to her feet, his arm supporting her. "What are you doing out here by yourself? Where's your mother?"

She shook her head, sobbing helplessly. Adam led her gently inside and switched on the hall light. All the doors stood open, and at first glance it was obvious the flat had been ransacked.

"You disturbed him?" Adam asked in dawning horror. "God, he could have killed you! Did you get a look at him?"

"No, he – he came out of the dark and spun me round. He – told me to get the spoons."

Adam frowned. "Spoons? What—?"

He broke off as Imogen came hurrying into the flat, her face anxious. "Adam, what's going on? You've left your lights on and the car door open – can't you hear the buzzer?"

She halted abruptly, eyes widening as she caught sight first of Mia, then of the state of the room.

"Look after her," Adam said brusquely. "I'm going to phone the police."

The two police officers, one of whom was a woman, arrived within minutes in an immediate response car, but Adam's hopes of a relatively swift return to order were soon thwarted.

"We can't get Scenes of Crime officers out till the morning, sir," the male officer told him apologetically. "CID will be taking charge then, but in the meantime, since it looks as though the whole flat's been done over, we'll have to seal it to preserve the scene." He paused, as the family stared at him blankly. "Is there somewhere else you could spend the night?"

Adam gave an exasperated sigh. "My brother's next door," he said tersely. "If it's really necessary for us to move out, I'm sure he'd put us up."

He phoned through while Mia, at the request of the woman officer, changed her clothes and handed over the jacket and skirt she'd been wearing for forensic examination.

Seeing the girl's bewilderment, PC Crossley explained, "Since he held you against him, there's bound to have been a transference of fibres. They could be important evidence when we catch up with him."

Then, while Adam stayed to answer the sergeant's questions, Mia and Imogen were escorted next door by PC Crossley. Louise met them, wearing a blue velvet housecoat.

"What a ghastly thing to have happened!" she exclaimed. She turned to Mia. "Are you sure you're all right, dear? You're very pale."

"It's the shock," Imogen replied. "She wasn't hurt, thank God. Louise, I'm so sorry to cause all this bother – you probably aren't even straight yet, after the move."

"Don't worry, we can manage. Russell's making up a camp bed in Rebecca's room and the guest room's just about usable. At least the bed's *in situ*." She turned to the police officer, who'd been standing silently while the formalities were exchanged.

"Sorry – you'll be wanting to interview Mia. Come into the sitting room. I've put the heating back on, and the kettle's boiling. Would you like tea, coffee or chocolate?"

When the three of them were settled with hot drinks and Louise had left them, PC Crossley turned to Mia. "I want you to tell me exactly what happened, from the minute you opened the front door."

Mia did so, repeating the intruder's words verbatim.

"He'd been looking for spoons?" The officer looked bewildered.

It was Imogen who replied. "I've been thinking about that; my husband, Adam Greenwood, is doing a series of television programmes here. The first went out last Thursday, and during the interview he mentioned owning a collection of Apostle spoons. They're quite valuable so it's possible the burglar was after those, but of course they're at our London home."

She smiled wryly. "I've always thought of Adam's audience as being semi-intellectual," she added. "It's a little surprising to find he's watched by the criminal classes!"

"I doubt if there's such a thing, Mrs Greenwood. It certainly seems possible that's what the man was referring to." Crossley turned back to Mia. "Was there anything that struck you about him? Close your eyes and try to think back. How tall was he? Did he have an accent? Was there any kind of smell about him – tobacco, perhaps? Was the hand over your mouth wearing a ring?"

Such information as Mia could supply seemed pitifully inadequate. "It all happened so quickly," she apologised. "I didn't see *anything* – not even how tall he was when he ran off, because I was blinded by Adam's headlights. But he bent down to speak in my ear, if that's any help, and his – yes, I remember now – his breath smelt of garlic."

"Well done!" said Crossley warmly, wondering how many hundreds in the town that would apply to. "What about an accent?"

Mia shook her head. "Hard to tell, when it's just a whisper. And I don't know if he had a ring, because he was wearing gloves."

When, finally, the police woman rose to go, they emerged from the sitting room to find Adam talking to Louise and Russell in the hall. Mia was escorted upstairs by her mother and Louise, and Rebecca, sitting up in bed agog with excitement, was strictly forbidden to question her until the morning.

The guest room was full of unpacked tea-chests and boxes, and since the radiator had only just been turned on, it felt chill. However the bed had hurriedly been made up and two hot-water bottles placed in it.

Wearily, Adam and Imogen began to undress. "No prizes for guessing how he got in," Adam commented, looking round for somewhere to put his clothes. "Through our bedroom window."

Imogen stared at him aghast. "I must have left it open when I went to lunch. I was in a hurry and I just didn't think."

"Even though we're on the ground floor?"

"But it was broad daylight and there are always people about here. I didn't know I'd be back late. Oh, Adam, I'm so sorry!"

"Which reminds me; where the hell were you?"

She explained about meeting Christina and offering to help out at the shop, but having established her whereabouts, Adam's attention had returned to the burglary.

"I can't believe this has happened – damn it, we've not been here a week!"

"But during that week you informed the nation of your valuable collection."

He nodded grimly. "That was brought home to me when I heard he was after 'the spoons'. The sergeant asked if I knew what he meant, and when I explained I got the impression he thought I'd brought it on myself."

"You did toss off the figure of twenty thou," Imogen reminded him.

"I didn't say *I* had a spoon worth that," he protested, "merely that it's the going rate for an outstanding example."

She shuddered. "Thank God you got back when you did. When Mia wasn't able to produce them, there's no saying what he might have done to her."

Adam drew her into his arms and kissed her hair. "I know, I know, it could have been much worse. Too bad we can't show Elliott and Maggie the flat, though; I gather we won't be allowed back till late afternoon, and then no doubt it'll need a good going-over to remove the fingerprint powder."

He patted her arm and released her. "In the meantime we'd better try to get some sleep; we've a busy day ahead of us."

Shivering with exhaustion, Imogen crept between the sheets of the strange bed and closed her eyes.

Five

Detective Superintendent David Webb stood at the window of Hannah's flat and stared out over the extensive gardens to the houses in the road behind.

"Can you actually see the Greenwoods' place from here?" he asked idly.

"No, it's along to the left, on the corner of Hunter's Hill. And they're on the far side of the road, so their garden doesn't come down this way. Why?"

"I hear they had a spot of bother last night – a break-in at one of the flats. The girl walked in on it, and had a nasty few minutes before friend Adam came to the rescue."

"*Mia*, you mean? His stepdaughter?"

"That's the one. I looked in at the station earlier, and John Baker was telling me about it. He's passed it on to Don, who's having a house-to-house done, but of course it was dark at the time, and the houses are all so widely spaced along there, it'll be a wonder if anyone saw anything."

"But is she all right? Was she hurt?"

"Oh, sorry love, is she one of yours? Don't worry, she seems none the worse, but she was threatened and held forcibly for a short time." He paused. "How old is she?"

"Coming up to sixteen."

"Poor kid; not a nice thing to happen." Webb seated himself in his usual chair. "They're having quite a baptism of fire, that household. John says one of the old girls in the maisonette witnessed a fatal RTA on Friday. Shook her up quite a bit."

"I can imagine. But to return to last night, how did an intruder manage to get into Fort Knox?"

Webb smiled. "You mean the electronic gates? All they do is prevent the theft of cars or large items. There's a small one alongside for tradesmen and pedestrians, which was no doubt how Chummie gained entry. I shouldn't be surprised if they put a lock on that, now."

"After the horse has bolted," Hannah observed.

"Quite. Though first impressions indicate nothing was taken."

"Then what was he after?"

Webb looked into his glass. "Did you catch the programme last week?"

"Yes, I was there. Gwen and I were invited to the studio."

He raised an eyebrow. "Lucky you. Well, I didn't see it myself, but I believe there was talk of some Apostle spoons?"

"*En passant.*"

"It seems Chummie was demanding 'the spoons', and received opinion is that's what he was referring to. Personally, I'm not convinced. I can't see him sitting down to watch a programme like Greenwood's, and even if he did, how the hell would he know where to find him?"

"I'm not sure I agree," Hannah replied. "Firstly, I presume you've no idea who 'Chummie', as you call him, is?"

Webb shook his head. "Not so far."

"Have you considered, for instance, that he might be an *aficionado* of those antiques programmes on TV? They're extremely popular, you know. Come to that, he could even be a collector himself. The fact that he didn't take anything else seems to show he was only interested in the spoons."

"It also shows," Webb put in a little tersely, "that he was interrupted."

Hannah conceded the point. "As to knowing where Adam Greenwood lives, there's been enough about it in the *News*, not to mention the fact that men have been working on the house for months. It would be easy enough to track him down."

"OK, OK," Webb said, putting up his hands. "Don Partridge might well have reached the same conclusion; I haven't spoken to him yet. Didn't you say they're doing a programme from the school?"

"Yes, a week on Thursday."

"Are you appearing in it?"

Hannah smiled. "Only in what might be termed 'crowd scenes'. Gwen will be interviewed, but the format is a look at education over the last five hundred years, so she'll only have her say right at the end."

"I must make a point of watching it." He paused. "You've met Adam Greenwood, then?"

"Only last Thursday – someone introduced us in the hospitality suite. Though Mia's a pupil, we've always dealt with her mother and, originally, her natural father."

"How did he strike you? Greenwood, I mean?"

"Oh, charm personified. A fascinating man, attractive, intelligent, volatile—"

"Hey, that'll do – I'm getting jealous! I thought he was supposed to be confrontational, rude and insensitive?"

Hannah smiled enigmatically. "But that's good television, isn't it?"

"You think it's a pose?"

"Not entirely; I'm willing to bet he has a temper, and probably makes no attempt to control it. But – and I know this sounds like a contradiction – I'd say he's capable of iron self-discipline when he needs it."

"Remind me not to ask you to analyse me!"

Hannah laughed. "You're a mass of contradictions, too."

It was true, she thought, looking across at him fondly. Though basically a compassionate man, he could be ruthless when it suited him. He was shrewd, but capable on occasion of surprising naivety; hard-headed, yet with an artistic gift that produced pleasing landscapes as well as startlingly lifelike caricatures. Even their relationship was two-sided: content, undemanding

67

friendship for long weeks, followed by urgent comings together which fulfilled a deep need in both of them.

It was fortunate, she reflected, that neither wanted marriage; David had been divorced when she met him, and for herself, her career had always come first. This arrangement was ideal, not only because they complemented each other so well, but because, having separate flats in the same building, they were able to keep their relationship secret – a vital consideration for a high-ranking police officer and the head designate of a private girls' school.

Which brought Hannah's mind back to her pupil. "To return to Mia, though, I hope she doesn't suffer any lasting ill effects. Gwen was saying the other evening that she's worried about her; she doesn't mix well and she's had an unsettling time since her parents' divorce."

"She'll be regarded as a heroine now," Webb commented. "Anyway, that's enough shop for a Sunday. I'd much rather speculate on the wonderful smell coming from the kitchen."

Hannah stood up. "A timely reminder; I must put on the vegetables."

Webb watched her leave the room, taking pleasure as always in her graceful movements and the fall of honey-coloured hair. With her oval face and wide, candid eyes she was unlike any headmistress he'd ever known, and he allowed himself a brief, amused comparison with the dragon who'd presided over his infant years before his thoughts returned, despite himself, to Greenwood and his spoons. Still, the affair was nothing to do with him; Don and his team would have everything under control. Which being the case, he told himself, getting to his feet, he would leave them to get on with it and put it out of his mind. And offer to open the bottle of wine for lunch.

Elliott Greenwood and Margo Devereux stood in the echoing emptiness of the flat above Adam's and looked about them.

"Well, there's plenty of space," Elliott said, breaking the silence. He walked to the far end of the room. "What's more, we've got a balcony, for drinks in the summer overlooking the garden." He bent forward to peer out of the window. "Good Lord, the cops are out there, too, ferreting among the undergrowth. Talk about looking for a needle in a haystack."

Margo shivered and hugged herself for warmth. "At least this flat shouldn't be as easy to break into," she said.

Elliott turned. "Oh, come on Maggie, it was a one-off – Adam opening his big mouth, as usual."

"But it's brought this house to public notice," Margo said. "There's sure to be a write-up in the local rag – it might give someone else ideas. Not," she added, "that it's anything to do with me."

Elliott walked back to her and put his arms round her. "Of course it's to do with you – what are you talking about? We share everything, remember? We both chose the colour scheme –" he glanced down at the emerald-green carpet which was the flat's sole attribute – "and we'll be furnishing it together, won't we? Not that we'll need much – I rather fancy the minimalist look."

"But we'll hardly be here," she objected, extricating herself from his embrace. "At least, I shan't. That's all I meant."

"It's not only for when we're performing in the area, you know; we can come down at weekends."

"You are joking, aren't you? You don't seriously imagine I'd contemplate driving out all this way just for the pleasure of camping here for a night?"

"Why not? Adam and Imogen intend to make full use of *their* flat. We could all—"

"That's different, they have to come to see their kids. Anyway, we see enough of Adam and Imogen in London."

Elliott's mouth tightened. "Please yourself," he said stiffly, "but I shall certainly be making use of it. It'll be great to see more of Ma and the family."

"*Viva* the Greenwood dynasty!" Margo declaimed.

It was perhaps as well that three short rings on their doorbell put an end to the discussion, and Adam's voice called through the letterbox, "Have you two finished up there? Louise says lunch is ready."

"Coming!" Elliott called back, and taking Margo's reluctant hand in his, he ran with her down the flight of stairs to the minute hallway and the side door which was their entrance.

Verity thought the new dining room splendid, and since, with both its leaves in, the table could accommodate twelve, there was room for everyone. A pity Naomi's previous engagement had kept kept her from joining them; otherwise, the whole complement of Greenwoods and Ryders would have been present.

As always, Louise had set the table beautifully, with newly unpacked china, crystal and silver. Verity was seated next to her, with Adam on her left and Elliott and Maggie directly opposite. Farther along, she saw that Tom and Mia had been placed together; according to Louise he was being very protective since her frightening experience, though from Mia's appearance she seemed to be unscathed. In fact, she was looking more animated than Verity had ever seen her.

This time last week, she thought, she'd been eating her solitary Sunday lunch in Oxford. What a lot seemed to have happened in the interim!

Russell, having poured the wine, proposed a toast: "To Greenwood, and all who live in it – including our part-time residents!"

They raised their glasses and drank.

"Have you decided what you'll need to bring down, Elliott?" Russell enquired.

"Oh, just the bare essentials, to start with. Unfortunately we've nothing spare at home, and the other problem is that we'll have to organise everything in a rush if it's to be ready for the tour. So we'll probably go round the auction rooms and pick up whatever's going in the way of bed, chairs, table and so on. Then, when we've more time, we can look for something more to our liking."

Margo was silent, toying with her cutlery and refusing to meet the glances Elliott threw in her direction. Verity's eyes moved from the beautiful, closed face to Elliott's with its strong brows and mobile mouth, the dark hair, less curly than Russell's, falling boyishly across his brow. Of all the male Greenwoods, including Tom, only Adam's hair was completely straight, taking after Eva rather than Max.

Had Elliott and Maggie had an argument? Verity wondered. She'd met the girl only once before, and been taken by her sparkling vivacity. It was certainly lacking today. She leant across the table.

"What do you think of the flat, Maggie?" she asked, and was amused at the instant transformation. Realising she had an audience, Margo's face lit up with a radiant smile. Every inch the professional, Verity thought drily.

"Oh, it's nice and spacious, and very well planned. But to be truthful, Mrs Ryder, when a place is empty I'm hopeless at picturing it furnished. I leave that leap of the imagination to Elliott." And at last she turned towards him, laying a hand charmingly over his. He covered it with his other hand, returning her smile.

"And the police presence is hardly a selling point," he added. "Do you know they're turning over the garden, Adam?"

"No, but I'm not surprised; the man escaped round the back, so they'll be looking for footprints or any other traces he might have left."

"And all because you boasted about those blasted spoons!" Elliott turned back to Margo. "Adam's always been obsessed by the Twelve Apostles."

Verity sensed rather than felt Adam stiffen at her side, and turned in time to catch a swift glance pass between him and Russell.

"All those lectures I suffered as a kid!" Elliott was continuing. " 'You can recognise St Thomas by his spear and St Matthias by his axe.' Right, Adam?"

Perhaps only Verity registered the slight pause before Adam

replied. "If the German system was used, yes. In the Italian, it's St Matthias who carries the spear."

Elliott put a hand theatrically to his brow. "I rest my case!" he declared.

"I don't remember St Matthias as one of the Apostles," Louise said with a frown.

"He replaced Judas Iscariot," Adam explained a little reluctantly, adding in spite of himself, "Come to that, Paul and Barnabas are also referred to as Apostles."

"My goodness!" Louise said lightly, "You *are* an authority!"

She rose to clear away the main course, helped by Rebecca. Adam immediately began a conversation with Tom across the table, possibly to forestall comment from Verity and thereby leaving her free to pursue her own thoughts.

What, in Elliott's teasing comments, had prompted that defensive stiffening? *Adam's always been obsessed by the Twelve Apostles.* Where was the harm in that? Hadn't Adam himself admitted as much during the programme? Was it, she wondered with a catch of her breath, because they now reminded him of Mr Morrison, whom he denied having met? And that quick exchange between Adam and Russell; what had she read in it? Complicity of some kind, certainly.

Verity was disturbed; she didn't care for the possibility of her son-in-law being involved in whatever linked Adam to the Apostles. And the resurrection, so to speak, of Mr Morrison reminded her of the unpleasant duty which awaited her tomorrow.

She looked up with a sigh to find Eva watching her from the opposite end of the table, and realised that her friend's thoughts must have been running on much the same lines, and with even greater unease. The two women exchanged smiles, and Verity felt marginally better. At least she could share her worries with Eva, as she had always done.

The telephone sounded out in the hall, and they heard Louise go to answer it. A minute or two later, she appeared in the doorway. "That was Lady Harwood. She's had the police round asking questions, and wanted to make sure we're all right. Wasn't that kind?"

"Sheer curiosity, more like," drawled Elliott.

Louise ignored him. "She's also invited us for drinks on Wednesday, to meet the neighbours. She apologised for the short notice, but they're going away at the weekend and she wanted to fit it in before she went."

"My goodness," Elliott said in mock awe, "you are moving in exalted circles. Too bad Maggie and I will miss out on it."

"Must you really leave this evening, darling?" Eva asked.

"We did invite them to stay," Russell put in. "The guest room will be available, but they insist they have to get back."

"My fault, I'm afraid," Margo apologised, with another dazzling smile. "I have a performance tomorrow evening and I'd prefer to spend the day quietly rather than the hassle of driving back. And one's never sure how long it will take, since it's impossible to gauge the traffic."

There was a general murmur of understanding.

"We'll be down again soon, though," Elliott added, with a half-defiant glance at his girlfriend, "with whatever furniture we've managed to collect in the interim. As I said, time's at a premium."

After the meal coffee was served in the sitting room, and as soon as they'd finished, Elliott and Margo stood up to go. A brief visit indeed, but it was to be hoped it had served its purpose.

It was a signal for the party to break up, and Verity was not sorry. Wine at lunchtime always gave her a slight headache, and the whole *forest* of Greenwoods could be rather overpowering. No doubt Maggie found the same.

As Eva closed their front door behind them, Verity said on impulse, "Tell me about those spoons."

Eva sighed. "They seem to be popping up all the time, don't they? If, of course, that's what the clergyman was talking about."

"It's certainly what everyone else is," Verity pointed out. "Adam said you and Max had a set?"

"Yes, I still have, I've just not unpacked them yet. But heavens, Verity, you must have seen – and used – them countless times! They were a wedding present and quite decorative, but nothing *that* special. To be honest, we never gave them much thought."

"But Adam did?"

"Yes; when he was about twelve he discovered you could distinguish one saint from another by what they were carrying. I confess I'd never even noticed they were different. Anyway, that was the start of it. Then one summer the school set them a project of their own choice, and much to our surprise, Adam plumped for Apostle spoons."

She smiled, remembering. "He spent most of that holiday cooped up in libraries or visiting auction rooms – not to buy, of course, but to examine what was on offer beforehand.

"He'd had crazes before, as all boys do, and we thought it would pass, but it didn't. So we bought him an antique spoon for his twenty-first birthday."

"Which did you give him?" Verity asked curiously.

"St Peter, with his bunch of keys."

"Has he got them all now?"

"Gracious no, only seven or eight. They really are pricey, you know, and obviously he has other priorities and commitments."

Including alimony and supporting his family, Verity thought.

"If you'd like to see mine, I'll root them out," Eva offered, "though our set is very run-of-the-mill compared with Adam's."

"Thanks, that would be interesting. In the meantime, I think I'll go up to my room for an hour or so. My head's throbbing, so I'll take an aspirin and perhaps have a short sleep."

"Good idea. I'll settle down with the Sunday papers."

Verity went slowly up the stairs, her mind still on the spoons. If she studied Eva's set very carefully, might she be able to unravel their mystery? Or did it exist only in her imagination? Was she making altogether too much of a dying man's words and her godson's reaction to them?

The morning had been bright, but by lunchtime it had clouded over and at three o'clock it started to rain.

Sonia stood at the kitchen window watching the steady downpour drench the garden, bending new leaves and spring flowers under its onslaught. She hated Sundays; it was a family day which everyone should spend together, and, though loath to admit it, it was the day she most missed Adam.

Impatiently she turned to the washing machine. She still had one more load to do, which included the clothes William had worn yesterday. Then she could get them ironed in time for him to take back with him tomorrow.

They'd had a good day out with Adam, it seemed. He had taken them to the Wildfowl Trust at Ringmere, in the south of the county, where they'd spent a fascinating day watching the birds and afterwards learning about their habitats in the Research and Education Centre.

Reluctantly, Sonia had to give her ex-husband full marks; it was not easy to find an activity that appealed equally to all three children. And to round off the day, he had driven home via Frecklemarsh where, to their delight, he had treated them to dinner at the fabled Gables restaurant. As a consequence, it had been nearly eleven when they reached home, and she was beginning to get anxious.

Before she and Adam moved to London they'd celebrated their wedding anniversaries at the Gables, but no doubt Adam had forgotten that. She thought briefly about its proprietor, Oliver Pendrick, and the talk there'd been when his second wife died. Still, he'd come through it all right and the restaurant still flourished, with clients coming from far and near.

Dismissing her memories, Sonia picked up an armful of clothes and was feeding them into the machine when something dropped to the floor. It was a gold pen, sleek and expensive-looking. She frowned and bent to pick it up, then, hearing footsteps running down the stairs, she called, "William!"

He appeared in the doorway, tall and lean and looking unnervingly like his father.

"What's this?" She held up the pen.

"Oh Lord, it's Dad's. He lent it to me yesterday, to make some notes. Oh *hell*! I'm meeting Pete and Steve in ten minutes, and that's the other side of town."

And he was leaving for Swindon first thing in the morning. There was a pause. William said tentatively, "Honestly, Mum, I don't know how I can get it back to him. I suppose you couldn't . . .?"

"I'm not," Sonia said firmly, "going to beard them all in that house of theirs."

"Well, could you drop it off at the studio? He said he'd be looking in there tomorrow. Or if you'd rather, I could ask him to call round here for it?"

"No," she said quickly, "if you borrowed it, it's your responsibility to see it's returned, not expect your father to collect it." She hesitated. The road where they lived led off the Marlton road, chosen specifically because of its proximity to both the high school and the grammar school. The television studios were some two miles farther on.

"Please, Mum!" wheedled William, sensing she was weakening.

"All right, I'll hand it in when I finish work. But you must phone him now, to tell him you have it. He probably thinks he's lost it somewhere."

"I'll phone from Pete's," William promised, and before she could remonstrate further, he added, "See you!" and slammed out of the front door.

Sonia laid the pen down on the counter, where it gleamed smugly in the rain-darkened room. For a minute she stood looking at it. Then she filled the powder container and switched on the machine.

*   *   *

76

It was unpleasant driving along the motorway, with spray from the large lorries misting their windscreen and their tyres whooshing on the wet road.

"They all seem very cosy down there," Margo said, breaking a long silence.

"Why do I get the feeling that comment is derogatory?"

"It strikes me as a little incestuous, that's all."

"Maggie, really! Lots of houses have granny flats these days."

"But with only one granny in them, and not a couple of brother flats thrown in for good measure. Oh, I'm not knocking it, really. Just as long as you don't expect me to engulf myself in it."

"Does this mean you're not happy about the flat?"

She said carefully, "I think it'll be great for when you're working in that area, which was how you sold me the idea. It was when you started talking about going down for weekends that alarm bells began to ring."

"But why? It's great to get away at weekends, especially in the summer."

"Yes, but not *there*! Oh God, how can I put this without upsetting you? I know you're close to your family – I suppose I rather envy you for that – but look at it from my point of view. Let's face it, I'm not one of them and they tend to – smother me. In the nicest possible way, of course," she added, smiling and coaxing him to do the same.

He didn't respond. She glanced sideways at the famous profile, noting the stubborn set of his mouth, his eyes fixed unwaveringly on the road ahead.

"Darling, don't be cross with me," she pleaded. She slid an arm round his neck, running her fingers up into his hair.

"If your intention is to send us straight under that lorry," Elliott remarked, "you're going the right way about it."

"Sorry. Rule One, don't distract the driver." There was a pause. "You *are* cross with me, aren't you?"

"More disappointed. I wanted you to be as enthusiastic as I am."

"But it's quite a distance to travel, isn't it? We can't go down till Sunday because of the Saturday performance, and then Monday's is already looming. We'd really have to go there and back in the day, like now, so we wouldn't actually be *staying* there at all."

"Well, I intend to get it sorted out as quickly as possible, and if there's time to spend a few days there before the Pinter rehearsals, I shall do so."

"Fair enough." Margo sat watching the rhythmic swish of the wipers, her thoughts bleak. When she'd first started seeing Elliott, her friends had warned against forming a relationship with one of the Greenwoods. "It's a case of 'love me, love my family'," they told her. "The Greenwoods don't come singly."

She'd not paid much attention. She and Elliott were in love and she was confident of her ability to hold on to him. She could cope with the occasional meetings with Adam and Imogen, though she'd little in common with either of them. But today at lunch, looking round the table at all the Greenwood faces, she had felt obscurely threatened, as though she were being required to sink her own personality and ambitions into one communal melting pot. It was stupid, of course; the family had shown her nothing but friendship.

Perhaps the root of it was her own possessiveness; she resented having to share Elliott's love on such a broad scale. But she did love him, and she wouldn't give him up to the family maw without a struggle. Which, in the short term, meant surrender.

She leaned over and kissed his cheek. "I'm sorry, darling, I'm just being silly. It's a lovely flat and we'll have great fun furnishing it, and I'll come down with you as often as I can."

And Elliott, having achieved his own way, relaxed into a smile. "That's my girl," he said.

Six

When Verity went down to make her toast the next morning, there was a small black box on the breakfast bar. She lifted the lid and saw, nestling amid the faded satin, Eva's Apostle spoons.

Almost superstitiously she lifted one out. She had no way of knowing which saint it represented, but the little figure held what looked like a staff. She studied it for a moment, turning it in her fingers, before replacing it and picking out the next one, and the next, until she had examined each of them in turn. One held an X-shaped cross, presumably St Andrew; one was carrying keys – also easy to recognise; another had a spear, which, according to Adam, could be either St Matthias or St Thomas, though she'd no idea how to differentiate.

"Ah, you found them!" said Eva's voice behind her.

"Yes, and you're right – I must have used them many times at your house, without really noticing them. Now I know they're specific representations, it makes them more interesting."

Eva lifted the kettle and filled it at the sink. "Did you sleep well?"

"Not particularly."

"Never mind, V, it'll soon be over. Ten o'clock, you said? We'd better leave at nine thirty to be sure of finding a parking place. We'll go in my car, you'll have enough on your mind without bothering about that."

Verity nodded, closing the lid of the box. "I think after all I'll just have a cup of tea," she said. "I'm not really hungry this morning."

"Try one slice," Eva urged her, sliding some bread into the toaster. "Life always seems worse on an empty stomach!"

"The girls wanted to come along, but I asked them not to. I said their being there would make me nervous. Which is true, though not for the reason they assumed."

"Who will be there, do you know?"

"Not really, except for the police and Mr Morrison's daughter and her husband."

The toast popped up. Eva buttered it, spread marmalade, cut it into triangles, and passed one slice to Verity. "Service with a smile! Sit down and have it here with me. We both need company today."

Verity noticed that despite her exhortation, Eva had forgone her egg this morning.

"Suppose it somehow comes out that he did know Adam?" she continued, sitting down at the breakfast bar.

"Do you think he did?" Verity countered.

"Oh God, V, I don't know. Adam was hiding something, I'm certain of that."

They ate their meagre repast in silence, and, still in silence, went upstairs to dress.

The Coroner's Court was a small, handsome room panelled in wood, with high windows – in case someone tried to escape? – and a raised dais on which the Coroner sat in a high-backed chair.

Catherine Poole, the dead man's daughter, was a woman in her forties, pale but composed. She answered the Coroner's questions in a clear but quiet voice. Her father's name was Eric George Morrison and he'd been seventy-two years of age. Since her mother's death he had lived with her and her husband at their home in Surrey – she gave the address. Yes, she'd identified him to the Coroner's Officer.

The Coroner leaned forward, surveying her over his spectacles. "Would you say, Mrs Poole, that your father tended to be absent-minded?"

"No, not at all. Quite the contrary."

"Might there have been something worrying him, then? Something preying on his mind that would account for his stepping off the pavement without checking first?"

She hesitated. "He *has* seemed preoccupied over the last week or two," she admitted after a minute, "but as he didn't confide in me, I assumed it concerned one of his parishioners."

The Coroner looked surprised, and she added, "Although he was retired, my father still helped out in the parish – taking occasional services, visiting and so on."

"And you've no idea what might have been causing him anxiety?"

"I'm afraid not, sir."

"His health was good?"

"For his age, very good, though he did suffer with arthritis."

A police sergeant then gave evidence concerning the length of the skid marks and the state of the road at the time of the accident, and confirmed that the car had undergone tests at the police workshop.

"A reconstruction was later done at the scene," he finished, "which showed that the vehicle was not exceeding the speed limit at the time of impact. Independent witnesses have confirmed this, and according to one statement the deceased apparently came from nowhere, straight into the path of the vehicle."

"Will these independent witnesses be called?"

"One of them, yes, sir: Mrs Verity Ryder."

Verity's name was called and she was shown into the court, Eva following and quietly taking a seat at the back. A quick glance round the court identified the couple who must be the daughter and son-in-law. She dreaded to think how they were feeling.

Yet again Verity gave her evidence, stressing that the driver of the car had had no chance of avoiding him.

The Coroner looked up from his papers. "Mrs – ah – Ryder,

the object of this inquest is to establish the cause of death, not to apportion blame. That will be dealt with in another court.

"Now, you say you saw Mr Morrison on the pavement minutes before the incident. Think carefully, if you would: could his actions in any way be construed as deliberate?"

Verity stared at him blankly, her heart pounding.

"I'm asking, Mrs Ryder, whether in your opinion Mr Morrison might have intended to end his life?"

She gasped. "Oh no, sir, not for a minute. He was deep in thought, that's all, and suddenly seemed to realise he was blocking the pavement. He mightn't even have appreciated he was stepping into the road – he just moved out of the way."

"And when you tended him before the ambulance arrived, did anything he said confirm that view?"

"He – wasn't really coherent, sir. He kept lapsing into unconsciousness." Verity prayed he would probe no further.

"So in your opinion the accident was the result of a momentary lapse of concentration on behalf of the deceased?"

Verity agreed, aware of overwhelming relief as the Coroner thanked her and allowed her to stand down. The inquest was then adjourned pending completion of enquiries, a burial certificate was issued and the body released to the relatives.

Verity and Eva made their way out of the court and were turning towards the main door when someone touched Verity's arm and she turned to see Catherine Poole and her husband.

"Mrs Ryder? I wanted to thank you for what you did for my father – it was extremely kind of you."

"Unfortunately, I wasn't able to do much," Verity replied.

"Look, I – don't want to impose on you, but I wondered if you and your friend would join us for a cup of coffee? I just feel I want to know absolutely everything that happened."

"Well, yes, of course, but there's little I can add to what I've already said." Verity could hardly refuse the request, but her alarm returned. Did this woman know more than she'd said in court? Was she going to be interrogated?

Mr Poole was saying quietly, "I think we'd all like to get out of this building. There's quite a reasonable café round the corner, where my wife and I had breakfast. Perhaps we could go there." He held out his hand. "I'm Tony Poole, by the way."

Eva was introduced in her turn and Verity briefly held her breath, but the name Greenwood seemed to mean nothing to the Pooles. Awkwardly, unsure what to say to each other, the four of them walked along Carrington Street and round the corner into Franklyn Road. The ambitiously named Blue Riband was some twenty yards along, and they seated themselves at a corner table. Coffee and cakes were ordered and Verity, to her shame, realised that she was ravenously hungry.

On closer inspection, Catherine Poole was quite attractive, with large grey eyes which bore signs of recent weeping. She smiled a little hesitantly.

"I do hope you don't feel we've press-ganged you. It's just that I still can't believe my father is dead."

"I understand," Verity assured her, "and I can at least put your mind to rest on one point; though it's hard to believe, considering his injuries, I really don't think he was in pain. He certainly gave no sign of it."

"Was he conscious when you reached him?"

"Yes, he – he apologised for causing the accident."

Catherine Poole's eyes filled. "How very like Father!"

Her husband patted her hand. "Did he say anything else?"

Verity hesitated, but the large, tear-filled eyes held hers beseechingly, and though aware of Eva's tension, she could not lie.

"He lost consciousness for a few minutes," she said slowly. "Then he suddenly gripped my hand and – and said quite distinctly, 'The Twelve Apostles.' "

The Pooles stared blankly at her, and Verity drew a tremulous breath of relief. It meant nothing to them. She'd done what she had to do, but it was all right, thank God.

The coffee and cakes arrived and were distributed. Then Mrs

Poole repeated incredulously, "The Twelve Apostles? What on earth did he mean by that?"

"I've no idea," Verity said truthfully.

"That was all?" Tony Poole asked, and Verity nodded.

His wife sipped her coffee. "There's another thing I don't understand; we were told there was a ticket in his pocket to some television programme."

Verity's hands clenched in her lap; she didn't dare look at Eva. Would this after all lead them to Adam? Oh God, she thought in panic, *why* did I mention the Apostles?

"I can't imagine why he wanted to see it," Mrs Poole was continuing, "or why he never mentioned it to us – but the point is, if that's what he came here for, why was he wearing his dog-collar? He never wore it on purely social occasions." She turned to Verity. "He *was* wearing it, wasn't he?"

Verity nodded. "Yes, I – tried to loosen it. That was when I realised he was a clergyman."

"The Twelve Apostles," Tony Poole said reflectively. "Had he preached a sermon on them recently, darling?"

"Not that I remember. And those were, as far as you know, his last words?"

"Yes; after that he closed his eyes again. He looked very peaceful, though."

Tony Poole passed round the plate of cakes and, feeling guilty, Verity took another. She was in need of its sustenance. Conversation began to flag, and Poole spoke of their children and the pleasure his father-in-law had taken in them.

Eventually, when there was nothing left to say, the little party broke up. Catherine Poole again took Verity's hand.

"Thank you so much for spending time with us. The truth is, I felt *I* should have been with Father when he died. Now, having heard exactly what happened, I almost feel I was. I'm sure your presence was a great comfort to him."

"I hope so," Verity said inadequately.

They parted outside the café, the Pooles turning in the direction of the station, Verity and Eva towards the car park.

"We could have done without that," Eva commented.

"Eva, I'm sorry I mentioned the Apostles, but I felt she had a right to know. I didn't realise they had the ticket to the show, though."

Eva squeezed her arm. "Don't worry about it; it meant nothing to them, that was obvious. I only hope that when they're given the ticket with his effects, they won't connect Adam's name with mine. If they do, it might seem odd we didn't pick up on their comment about the programme."

Sonia saw Adam just ahead of her as she approached the studios and called his name, but he didn't hear her. She quickened her steps, following him across the forecourt of the building and through the revolving door. Here, her progress was barred by a doorman, who enquired her business.

"I'm Mrs Greenwood," she said hurriedly, gesturing towards Adam, who was now being handed an envelope by a girl at the reception desk.

"Have you any identification, madam?"

"Oh, for heaven's sake!" she exclaimed impatiently, afraid Adam would vanish before she could catch him. She fumbled in her bag for her driving licence and was at last allowed to proceed. To her relief, Adam had taken the envelope over to a window, where he tore it open and began to read the contents.

She removed the gold pen from her handbag and approached him.

"Adam—"

He gave no sign of having heard her.

"Adam!" she said again, a little louder. He turned then, slowly, as though in a daze, and she was shocked by the sight of his face. All the blood had drained away and his eyes were blank, regarding her totally without recognition.

"Adam, what is it? Are you ill?"

He gave a negative movement of the head, not so much a shake as an attempt to clear it, and the envelope fluttered to the floor. Sonia bent to retrieve it, noting that it was addressed in an elderly hand to *Adam Greenwood, Esquire – By Hand.* He made no attempt to take it from her.

Seriously alarmed now, she said urgently, "Adam, it's Sonia. Are you all right?"

To her untold relief his eyes suddenly focused. "Sonia," he repeated, and wiped a hand across his brow. As though suddenly becoming aware of them, he looked down at the sheets of paper, folded them quickly and stuffed them into his pocket. Then, in almost his normal voice, he asked, "What are you doing here?"

She'd forgotten herself, but she held up the pen. "William borrowed it – didn't he phone you?"

He took it from her, shaking his head, and she silently cursed the carelessness of youth.

"Look, I think you should sit down; you seem to have had a shock. I'm sure someone—" She turned in search of help, but to her surprise he caught hold of her arm.

"Don't go, Sonia, please."

"I was only trying to see if—"

"I don't need anyone else, if you'll just stay for a while."

He made an effort to pull himself together. "But of course you have other things to do. I'm sorry, I mustn't—"

"I'll stay if you want me to," Sonia said, aware of the thunderous beating of her heart. When had Adam last needed her? Somewhere in the mists of time.

"I've no right—" he began.

"Don't be ridiculous." She tried to be sensible for both of them. "Have you an appointment here? William said—"

"Nothing definite."

"Well, I think you should rest for a while. My car's outside; if you'd like to come back with me and have a brandy or something, you'd be very welcome."

She didn't expect him to agree, but he said meekly, "That sounds an excellent idea. Thank you."

She took his arm and they walked back across the foyer to the revolving doors where, this time, the doorman touched his cap to them. Sonia's thoughts were whirling. What on earth was she going to do with him? Ought she to call a doctor? He still seemed in a state of shock.

The car was parked on a yellow line; she'd taken the risk, expecting only to be a minute, and luck was still with her. She reversed in a handy driveway and drove back down the Marlton road to her own turning, trying to remember if either Bethany or Seb had said they'd be back for lunch.

But the front door was locked and there was no sign of them. Sonia wasn't sure whether to be pleased or not. She showed Adam into the living room and went to the cupboard where she kept drinks for the few occasions when she entertained, including some brandy she'd brought home from France. She poured him a stiff measure and handed it to him.

"Have you had any lunch?" she asked.

"No, but I—"

"I was going to make myself an omelette."

"That sounds tempting." He looked up at her with a wry smile. "I remember your omelettes."

She left him, her mind spinning, and prepared the meal on auto-pilot, laying a tray with bread and butter and some fruit before sliding the golden, fluffy omelettes on to the plates.

They ate at the coffee table, hardly speaking, but at least he finished everything she'd laid before him, and some colour began to come back into his face.

She said tentatively, "Adam, I don't know what's wrong, but if there's anything I can do—?"

"No," he said. "There's nothing anyone can do."

He drank the last of the brandy and set the glass down. "And what's worse," he added, "there's nothing I can do, either, God help me."

His voice cracked and he put a hand across his eyes. Without thought Sonia dropped to her knees in front of him and gathered him into her arms. He made no attempt to resist and after a moment he put a reciprocal arm round her. She held him close, conscious of his laboured breathing and his almost tangible tension, while she murmured words of comfort and endearment as she would to one of the children, silly, formulaic words that meant nothing but seemed to help: "There, there, it'll be all right. Try not to worry."

After several minutes his breathing quietened and his arm fell away. She sat back on her heels, looking up into his face as he gazed back at her. He put out a hand and gently touched her cheek, and she knew that, in that moment at least, he wanted her. Knew, too, that if he put his desire into words, she would go to him. Then he gave a deep sigh and she accepted, with bitter regret, that the moment had passed.

He stood up slowly, holding out a hand to help her to her feet, and she released it as soon as she was upright.

He said, "I'm sorry I can't explain, love. Sufficient to say you were my salvation just now. You helped me through *un mauvais quart d'heure*, and I'm most grateful."

She could think of nothing to say that wasn't a platitude.

"Bless you," he said, and, bending forward, kissed her on the cheek. Then, leaving her standing there, he let himself out of the house.

Flinging herself down on the chair he'd just vacated, Sonia burst into a storm of tears.

Verity picked up her phone to hear Naomi's voice. "I've been thinking about you today," she said. "How did the inquest go?"

"It was pretty unnerving, actually. We had coffee with Mr Morrison's daughter and son-in-law afterwards, which dragged it out rather."

"Couldn't you have refused?"

"Not really; she desperately needed to know what happened."

"Well, at least you can relax now. How was the lunch party?"

"Most enjoyable, it was a pity you couldn't join us. Louise pulled out all the stops, as usual." Then, afraid that might sound like a criticism, Verity hurried on, "I suppose you won't have heard about Saturday night? Mia returned home to the empty flat in the middle of a burglary."

"My God! Was she hurt?"

"No, but only because Adam came back in the nick of time. The man was trying to force her into the house."

"That's frightful. Did he get away with much?"

"No, as it happens, he didn't take anything." Verity hesitated, but Louise was sure to mention it. "It seemed he was looking for Adam's Apostle spoons."

There was a long silence. "Naomi?"

"Yes – I heard. A rather specialised burglary, wasn't it?"

"We think it must have been someone who saw the programme and assumed Adam kept them here. They're in London, of course, under lock and key."

"Have you any idea who it might have been?"

Verity gave a short laugh. "Not being on nodding terms with criminals, darling, no, I haven't."

"I meant – have the police found anything to link to him?"

"Heaven knows; if they haven't, it won't be for lack of trying. They were in the flat most of the day, while their colleagues prowled round the garden with tweezers and tapes."

"You've had an eventful first week in Shillingham, haven't you? Let's hope things settle down a bit from now on."

When Naomi had put the phone down she stood for several minutes, deep in thought. Saturday. The day Nigel had vanished; Nigel, who had been so contemptuous and scathing about the Greenwoods. Surely he wouldn't have—? He wasn't above a bit of petty thieving, as she knew to her cost. He'd taken her silver cigarette lighter with him, a souvenir of her smoking days, as well as a Crown Derby ornament of which she'd been quite fond. They'd bring him a few pounds, no doubt – a fraction of their real value.

But breaking into a flat and manhandling a young girl: surely even Nigel wouldn't stoop to that?

Even Nigel? her brain repeated. This was the man who'd been under her roof for the best part of six months, who'd shared her bed more than once. Surely she wasn't now prepared, without a shred of evidence, to cast him in the role of dyed-in-the-wool villain?

Hell hath no fury? She gave an angry laugh, admitting that it rankled that he'd left as she was on the point of giving him notice; wishing, childishly, that she'd got it in first.

No, the whole idea was ridiculous and she wouldn't entertain it for a minute. Nevertheless, she'd be glad when the thwarted burglar was apprehended. At least, she hoped she would.

Hannah put the timetables in the desk drawer and sat back in her chair. The boarders were returning tomorrow and on Wednesday the new term would begin, her last as deputy head. For when Gwen and her husband flew off to Canada in August, Hannah's long-term ambition would be realised and she'd become headmistress of Ashbourne School for Girls.

She was looking forward to the challenge, confident of her own ability. She had, after all, been in charge during Gwen's sabbatical and had enjoyed the experience. This time there would be no set time limit, no inevitable handing back of the reins; she'd be free to put into effect all the ideas which she'd had during that year and most of which Gwen had vetoed on her return.

Until Gwen's startling announcement last summer that, in her late forties, she had fallen for a Canadian professor and was about to marry him, the status quo had seemed set to continue until either Gwen retired or Hannah moved to pastures new, which she was loath to do. Ashbourne had always been a part of her life as it had of Gwen's, since both had attended it as girls, though not as contemporaries. And until Gwen's return from Canada, the two of them had worked well in harness. The few ripples there had been since were caused, as Hannah readily admitted, by her own reluctance to give up her temporary authority.

She locked her desk drawer and stood up. One of the first events of the term would be the Greenwood broadcast. She hoped it wouldn't cause too much disruption.

Hannah smiled as she gathered her things together, remembering David's reaction to her comments about Greenwood. And from Adam, her thoughts turned naturally to Mia. This term she'd have her stepcousin Rebecca in her class; Hannah hoped the two girls got on well and would support each other.

Her mind already in gear for the coming term, she set off for home.

In the unexpected eruption of her feelings for Adam, Sonia had forgotten the envelope whose contents had caused him such distress. It was only later that afternoon, as she searched for a handkerchief in her jacket pocket, that her fingers encountered its crumpled corners and she drew it out, frowningly examining the spidery writing. Not many people used 'Esquire' nowadays. She turned the envelope over, and was surprised to see the name of the Tivoli Hotel stamped across the flap. Who could Adam possibly know who would stay there?

Might it be a fan letter? He'd received some fairly vitriolic ones in the past, but they'd never bothered him. His maxim had been, "As long as they talk about the programme, it doesn't matter what they say."

But whatever that letter contained, its effect had been traumatic. News of someone's death? Possibly, though why, if the writer had been staying at the Tivoli, hadn't he approached Adam in person?

Sonia sighed, smoothing out the creased envelope with her fingers. Then, mocking herself as she did so, she took it up to her bedroom and slipped it under a pile of jumpers in one of the drawers. An odd souvenir, admittedly, but it would remind her

91

of the precious few minutes she'd spent with Adam. No doubt they would have to last her a long time.

At nine o'clock that evening, as he was putting the finishing touches to a watercolour begun *in situ* the previous weekend, Webb received a phone call from the Chief Superintendent.

"Trouble, Spider," Fleming's voice said in his ear. "Some bones have been uncovered in Fox Woods – almost definitely human remains. Ledbetter's out there with Stapleton, but a more senior police presence is required. No point setting off now – it's black as pitch out there – but give them the once-over in the morning, will you, and report back?"

"Of course, sir. Have we any more details?"

"Precious few. A couple walking their dog found them – at least, the dog did. Been there some time from initial reports, but the path, lab will tell us more. Once we have an idea of the age, we'll access all the relevant misper files."

Webb sighed; missing persons were always a minefield; any enquiries about them, no matter how long after the person had disappeared, resurrected hope or despair on the part of relatives, who frequently had to be told later that it was someone else anyway.

"I'll get on to it first thing in the morning, sir."

Fox Woods, Webb thought, as he washed his brushes and put his paints away. A good hiding-place for a body, as had been amply demonstrated. In instances like this, he reflected, they usually uncovered more metaphorically than they did physically: long-forgotten secrets, family resentments and betrayals. It would be interesting to see what came to light in this case.

Seven

The rain had cleared away and the April morning was luminous, a pale sun glinting on wet foliage and wreathing the fields in a gossamer mist. Just the morning, Webb thought philosophically, for digging up old bones.

Fox Woods were over an hour's drive from Shillingham, being located some ten miles north-west of Steeple Bayliss, on the borders of Gloucestershire. The Ordnance Survey showed little by way of habitation in the vicinity, just one small hamlet by the name of Foxwell, comprising a handful of farms and cottages.

DS Marshbanks was his driver this morning; it felt strange to have anyone other than Jackson with him, but Ken had recently been promoted to inspector and in any event was working on a case of his own. Though they didn't meet as frequently as before, Millie still ensured that Webb had plenty of opportunities to see his godson.

Marshbanks, also newly promoted, was a nice lad who, during his five years in CID, had learned to curb his ebullience while still throwing himself heart and soul into the job. Though his public school contacts – which on occasion had proved useful – were initially derided by his colleagues, he'd long since been accepted as one of their own. Today, he had the added advantage of coming from Steeple Bayliss, so knew the area better than most of the Shillingham men.

"What are these woods like, Simon? It's years since I was up there."

"I've not been lately myself either, Guv, not since we used to bike over as kids. But they cover quite a large area, with some parts more popular than others. The local schools have nature rambles there – you know, naming trees and birds, going out to see the first bluebells and so on."

"Then we can be thankful it wasn't a nature class that found the bones. Which is our best route?"

"The SB bypass, then cross-country through Popplewell and Foxwell. Unless you want to call at the station first?"

"No, DI Ledbetter will meet us at the scene."

It was still only eight thirty when they turned off the ring road along a B-road signposted 'Popplewell'. Some years ago, Webb recalled, they'd rescued a girl from a local farm, after – to his considerable sceptism – being directed there by a dowser. Ah well, he was beyond being surprised these days.

After leaving the village there was another stretch of open country before, off to the right, they passed the collection of buildings known as Foxwell, and by then they could see the dark shape of the woods spreading along the skyline.

Marshbanks drew up behind a line of official cars and a uniformed constable came to meet them.

"Superintendent Webb and DS Marshbanks. Is DI Ledbetter here?"

"PC Simpson, sir. Yes, he asked me to take you straight to him."

They ducked under the blue and white police tape and followed Simpson along a taped route through the trees which grew progressively more dense. Off the path, clumps of primroses lay like patches of sunlight among the dark undergrowth. Precious little to be gained by an in-depth search along here; the murderer – if murderer there were – would be long gone, and all his traces with him. Their only hope of a lead would be in the bones themselves and their shallow grave.

Voices reached them first, and as the trees gradually parted they emerged into a clearing where the gruesome work was in progress. Several men were grouped round a shallow grave, some of them on their knees, gloved hands in the soil, while a video camera recorded the scene.

DI Ledbetter turned at their approach. A strikingly handsome man with corn-gold hair and blue eyes, he looked more like a male model than a policeman – an advantage, as Webb acknowledged, since villains were disinclined to take him seriously.

"Superintendent!" He came forward to shake Webb's hand, formal in the presence of their subordinates. "And DC Marshbanks, isn't it? We've met before."

"DS as of last month," Webb corrected.

"My congratulations. Now, let me show you what we've got."

They walked over to the group. Alongside the hole a large plastic sheet had been spread to receive the excavated soil, and a couple of sieves and a trowel lay on top of it. A wooden box lined with cloth contained a pile of bones, among them a skeletal hand and what looked to Webb's untutored eye like a femur.

"The Cornoner's Officer was here last night," Ledbetter was saying, "and Dr Stapleton also looked in. Wouldn't commit himself as to how long they've been here; we'll have to wait for the path. results. Chances are, though, it's less than seventy years."

Which was the time limit below which police investigation was required into the identity of the remains and the cause of death.

"You can bet your life," Webb agreed, "even if it turns out to be sixty-nine! Let's hope for much less, or we'll be overwhelmed with mispers. Any clue as to gender?"

"Male – that's about all we do know. Part of the pelvis was unearthed last night."

"What time was this discovered?"

"The call was logged just after seven. By the time I arrived it was almost dark here under the trees." He glanced up at the lacy canopy through which the strengthening sunlight now filtered. "We set up lights and removed everything that was visible, then secured the scene and left the rest till this morning."

"Have the people who discovered them made a statement?"

"Hawkins is going round there this morning; fortunately, they live in SB."

"A couple walking their dog, wasn't it?"

"In a manner of speaking; they were actually in the car when the dog needed to be let out, but as they put on its lead, it wriggled free and took off into the woods. By the time they caught up with it, it was yapping and worrying at the bones."

The men who'd been sifting the soil by hand sat back and their companions took over again, each spadeful being meticulously shaken through a sieve onto the plastic sheet. Lucky the Broadshire soil was so loamy, Webb thought, as he had on similar occasions before.

"When's Stapleton going to examine them?" he asked.

"This afternoon, two thirty."

"I'll stay on, then; might as well have as much info as possible to report back."

He looked about him at the encircling trees, the ground still wet and muddied by footprints.

"No conceivable chance, I suppose, of natural causes? Someone collapsing and dying, and being gradually covered with earth and leaves?"

Ledbetter shook his head. "He might have died naturally, but he didn't bury himself. This is a man-made grave all right."

"Sir!" Both officers turned. One of the men was holding up a sieve. "We've struck lucky with this spadeful – shreds of clothing and a coin or two, probably from his pocket when it disintegrated."

"Can you make out the date on them?"

The man picked out a blackened disc and turned it over. "It's covered with verdigris. Post-decimalistation, though, judging by its size – if it's British, that is." He spat on the coin, rubbed it on his sleeve and examined it again. "Yes, here we are – nineteen . . . seventy-two."

"Well done!" Ledbetter exclaimed, holding out his hand for the coin. "How long do they stay in circulation, anyone any idea?"

"Until they're damaged or updated, I should think," offered Marshbanks, who'd been squatting down talking to the men.

"At least it gives us a starting point. Anything else?"

Another man had been rubbing the lumps of soil in his sieve. "Yes, there's some buttons – off a shirt, by the look of them – and something which might have been a wallet. No credit cards, unfortunately. They'd have been indestructible – must have been removed before he was buried."

"They didn't exist in seventy-two," Webb said. "So there's nothing that might identify him?"

"Sorry, sir, not even a watch. Hold on, though – here's something else. Looks like a bow tie!" He held it up, dark, sodden and barely recognisable. "Well, what do you know?"

"Any label?"

"Sorry, sir."

Webb watched as the findings were dropped one by one into specimen bags. "Well, at least we've narrowed it to under thirty years, but a hell of a lot of people must have disappeared since seventy-two."

"And if he was a tramp or a drop-out, he wouldn't have been reported missing anyway."

"Thanks," Webb said drily, "a little encouragement is never out of place."

Ledbetter grinned. "Just facing the facts, Dave. Well, there's not much we can do here; I think I'll leave the boys to it and head back to SB. Care to join me for a pint later at the Barley Mow?"

Webb nodded. "Fine. One o'clock? Then we can go straight on to the morgue. With only a handful of bones it'll be less stomach-churning than usual."

Catherine Poole sat down at the kitchen table with the latest batch of condolence letters and steeled herself to read them. Though it was wonderful to know how widely loved her father had been, the expressions of gratitude for his kindnesses unfailingly made her cry. He had been a friend as well as a clergyman to his parishioners, and even after he'd retired, the older ones in particular had continued to go to him with their troubles rather than to the new vicar, who was young and rather brash.

The names of the letter writers brought back some of her earliest memories: Madge and Henry Piper, regular dinner guests at the vicarage in the old days; Tessa Blaise, a friend since schooldays; George Parker, a former churchwarden whose family had moved away. Then there were less personal notes and cards, many from couples her father had married or whose children he had baptised, but each with his or her own reason to mourn him.

Catherine gathered the day's post into a pile for Tony to read on his return from work. Then she topped up the dozen or so flower vases containing more tributes – glorious, exotic blooms alongside sprays of spring flowers. How kind people were.

Finally, when she could delay it no longer, she went up to her father's study-bedroom. The prospect of going through his things filled her with dread. She knew that if she waited till the weekend Tony would help her, but she felt obscurely that she was trespassing, and one trespasser might be more acceptable than two.

His clothes she could not, for the moment, bear to look at, but the papers should be checked as soon as possible, in case any of them needed attention. Catherine went to his desk and stood for a moment, hands resting on the polished surface as she looked at the photographs arrayed there: her mother, taken just before she became ill, looking so alive and dearly familiar; she and Tony on their wedding day; recent snaps of the children.

Slowly she lowered herself on to the red leather chair, a little cracked and dented after many years' service, and pulled open the bottom drawer which contained his filing system. The green folders suspended from their rail were all neatly labelled: Utilities, Medical, Pensions, Insurance, Banking, Legal. Painstakingly she pulled out one after another and went through them, noting with relief that nothing needed to be done other than notifying the various companies of the death, which was already in hand.

Her father had always been methodical, and Catherine knew everything of importance would be in those files. Still, if she did a quick check of the other drawers while she was here, it would be another task to cross off the list.

The top one contained some rough notes for sermons, a few old service sheets, an assortment of ballpoint pens and some stationery. She pushed it shut and opened the middle drawer, expecting that its contents, too, would be of little interest.

To her surprise, though, she discovered a neat pile of envelopes, addressed, stamped and sealed. Curiously she picked them up and flicked through them – ten in all. Three were destined for overseas, two addressed to university professors and another to a member of parliament, but she couldn't recall her father speaking of any of them.

Catherine tapped her fingers thoughtfully on the desk. Why was Father writing to these people and, more to the point, why hadn't he posted the letters? Had he intended doing so on his return from Broadshire? If only she knew why he'd gone there, why he'd attended a television programme, why he'd been wearing his dog-collar, his death might make some sense. His briefcase, the only luggage he'd taken with him, had offered no clue, containing only his pyjamas, sponge bag and library book.

She bit her lip, wrenching her mind back to the envelopes. Perhaps they were connected with his charity work – an appeal of some kind. Ought she to add a note advising the recipient of his death? But it would involve opening the letters, and she shied away from that. Better just to post them, and deal with any responses as and when they were received.

She carried the envelopes downstairs, checked in the hall mirror that her eyelids didn't look too swollen, and set off for the pillar-box at the end of the road.

*   *   *

Rebecca said apprehensively, "I hope I'll like this new school."

"I'm sure you will, darling," Louise assured her. "And you'll have Mia in your class, so she can show you the ropes."

Rebecca glanced slyly at her brother. "What's she like, Tom? I've never heard her say more than half a dozen words."

"With you around, she wouldn't have had the chance!" he retorted.

"Oh come on, she is exceptionally quiet – admit it."

"She's shy. She'll be fine when she gets to know you."

"Are you seeing her today?"

He pulled a face. "No, she's got to finish packing, and she goes back this afternoon."

"At least I'm not boarding," Rebecca said thankfully. "I'd *hate* it."

"I don't think Mia likes it much, either."

"Then why doesn't she go to day school in London?"

"How should I know?"

"She's always been at Ashbourne," Louise put in, "and I suppose when her mother married Adam, they thought it would be less unsettling for her to stay there."

"Anyway," Tom remarked to his sister, "you're not the only one going to a new school, and I won't have Mia to hold my hand."

Rebecca laughed. "I bet she'd rather hold your hand than mine."

Louise switched on the dishwasher. "Tom, if you're not seeing Mia, why don't you take Rebecca to the sports centre for a game of tennis? You should be outdoors, both of you, on a day like this."

He pushed himself away from the table. "Like a game, Sis?"

"OK, and we can stop off for a pizza on the way home. It is our last day of freedom, after all."

"All alone?" Russell asked, coming into the kitchen to find his wife rolling pastry.

"Yes, I packed them off to the sports centre." She paused. "They were voicing doubts about their respective new schools. I do hope they'll settle in, Russ."

He kissed her cheek. "Of course they will. They're adaptable, both of them."

"But it's a crucial time for them, with GCSEs and A-levels looming."

"Exactly; they'll have a term to settle down, then they'll be in at the beginning of the syllabus. We discussed all this when we were timing the move, remember."

Louise sighed. "Yes, I know. I told Rebecca Mia would be a help, but I'm not so sure."

"Why?" Russell leant over and helped himself to a piece of raw pastry trimming.

Louise smacked his hand away. "You're as bad as the children! Well, she's an odd girl, isn't she? Half the time I don't think she's aware of what's going on around her."

"She seems to have come out of her shell with Tom, though," Russell commented. "Chip off the old block, my son!"

"Actually, you're right. And to give her due, she took that attack in her stride."

"Yes." Russell frowned. "Odd thing, that. Do you really think it was down to old Adam shooting off his mouth about his spoons?"

"What other explanation is there?"

"Well, it's a large house, therefore reasonably wealthy inhabitants. Perhaps, seeing that end of it in darkness, someone just decided to try his luck. For all we know, burglaries might be run-of-the-mill in this area."

"Are you going to put a lock on the wicket gate?"

"It'd be a hell of a bind, having to go out to collect the post or let the window cleaner in."

"We could have post boxes at the gate, like they do in the States."

"Well, I'm not convinced. It was probably a one-off, there's no point in overreacting." He looked at his watch. "What time's lunch, by the way? I have to go into the studio this afternoon to start planning the trip."

"Any dates for it yet?"

"End of June. Best time for the Andes."

"Lucky devil!"

"My love, it's not a holiday, as I tell you every time. It's hard slog, believe me, sitting around for hours to get the right shots, as often as not freezing cold and soaking wet."

"My heart bleeds for you," Louise said, fitting the pastry expertly over the pie dish. "Right, lunch in half an hour, then."

"And don't worry about the kids," he said, on his way out of the room. "They'll be fine."

This time last week, Louise thought, they had all just arrived and were in the throes of unpacking. Thank God they hadn't known what the next seven days would hold – Mother witnessing that accident, Mia being attacked. It hadn't been an auspicious start to their living here.

It was strange that Mother hadn't wanted either Naomi or herself to accompany her to the inquest; Louise had been a little hurt that Eva'd been chosen in her stead, even if she *was* Mother's oldest friend. Which was childish, she told herself severely. And thinking of Naomi reminded her that she must ring and fix that meal.

Washing the flour off her hands, Louise set about preparing lunch.

The verdict on the bones was not as conclusive as Webb had hoped, and by the end of it he knew little more than he had before. It was impossible, Stapleton had insisted, to judge the age of the deceased accurately. However, taking into account degenerative change and the amount of wear on the teeth, the likelihood was that he'd been a young man. Probable height about five-ten, slender build and fair-haired, judging by the few hairs still adhering to the skull.

There was, as Webb had feared, no obvious cause of death, and no positive dating. Thank God for the coins, he thought devoutly. And now the skull was on its way to act as a prototype for facial reconstruction. It was uncanny how true to life those likenesses could be.

Meanwhile such description as they had would be circulated through police publications, but it would be a long time before anything came through. Records weren't computerised in the seventies, so it would be a question of digging out old files and searching through the archives, a mind-bendingly tedious operation. There were advantages, he thought with a wry grin, to being a superintendent.

He glanced at Marshbanks in the seat beside him. When Webb had joined Ledbetter for lunch, he'd given the sergeant a couple of hours off, and had a pretty good idea how he'd spend them.

"Call in at home, did you?" he asked now.

"Yes, Guv. Mum was quite chuffed to see me."

"And are they all well?" Webb had met the Marshbanks during the course of an investigation four years ago – the same, as it happened, that had involved the dowser he'd been remembering earlier.

"Fine. My sister's having another baby – that'll make three! Mum's in her element."

A nice, uncomplicated family, the Marshbanks. In his line of business, he didn't come across many like that. He leant forward and switched on the radio.

"Let's see if they mention the excavation on the news."

They did: "Some human remains have been discovered in Fox Woods in north-west Broadshire," the unemotional voice of the announcer informed them. "A post-mortem was unable to establish cause of death, which is believed to have occurred between twenty and thirty years ago. The remains are those of a young, slimly built man. Police are asking for any information which might help in identifying him. The number to ring—"

Webb switched off the radio. "They were quick off the mark –

it's barely an hour since the press conference. Just as well I phoned the Chief Super from SB, he wouldn't have thanked me if he'd heard it first on the radio."

Imogen caught the headlines as she was driving home after an exhausting half-hour helping Mia move into her new room at Ashbourne.

The boarding houses, Austen and Brontë, were positioned adjacent to each other in Montpellier Gardens, a little farther round the crescent than the school itself, and as always Imogen was impressed by their graceful Georgian architecture. Each house stood in its own grounds and accommodated some fifty girls. Mia was in Austen, and this term she'd been allocated one of the double rooms, an improvement on last term's dormitory.

Imogen had taken the opportunity for a word with Miss Fowler, the housemistress, about last Saturday's episode. She was a sensible woman and would keep an eye on Mia, though, Imogen had to admit, the experience had not seemed to distress the girl too much. She suspected she had young Tom Greenwood to thank for her daughter's swift recovery.

"We'll still be in Shillingham for your first exeat," she'd told Mia as she was leaving, "so I'll phone Daddy nearer the time and arrange for you to come to us instead."

To her surprise, Mia had demurred. "But he'll be expecting me, and he promised to take me to the cinema again."

"Darling, I thought you weren't very happy about going there?" Imogen protested, not sure how to take this volte-face.

"It was much nicer last time, and Rosie's quite sweet now."

"Just as you like, of course," Imogen said, trying not to feel rebuffed.

When she arrived home, Adam was sitting reading the paper. "My daughter's undergoing a sea-change," she commented, taking off her jacket.

"How so?"

"For one thing, she opted to go to Scott's instead of here for her next exeat, and for another, I can't believe how unfazed she's been about that intruder business."

"She's growing up, that's all. I suppose the police haven't been in touch about the break-in?"

"No, but I hardly expected them to. And they'll have more important things on their mind now."

He looked up. "What do you mean?"

"I heard on the car radio that some 'remains' have been found in a wood near Steeple Bayliss, which I bet will push our intruder on to a back burner.

"I don't know about you," she continued, picking up her jacket, "but I'm ready for a cup of tea. It's hard work carting all that stuff up two flights of stairs. If I'd known you'd be back early, I'd have roped you in to help."

She glanced at her husband, but he'd returned to his paper and made no reply. Men! she thought whimsically, and went to put the kettle on.

Eight

C hristina French glanced across to where Imogen was working competently on one of the room settings. That had always been her forte; she had a flair for juxtaposition, unexpectedly contrasting wallpaper and fabric, carpets and furniture, into a harmonious and at the same time original whole.

Seeing that the young assistant was serving a customer, she strolled over, wondering how to voice tactfully what was on her mind.

"You said Adam was out with his children on Saturday," she began – casually, she hoped. "I was wondering, does he ever see his ex-wife?"

Imogen looked up in surprise. "Not if either he or she can help it. She usually arranges to be out when he picks them up and delivers them."

"They don't meet socially, then?"

"God, no!" Imogen gave a small, exasperated laugh. "It's obvious you don't know much about divorced couples, Christy!"

"I just wondered," Christina said vaguely, accepting the criticism, if that is what it was. But her sense of unease deepened. Did she owe it to Imogen to tell her that at lunchtime on Monday she'd seen Adam Greenwood being driven down the Marlton road by his ex-wife? Or was discretion the best policy? As Imogen said, Christina had little experience in these matters. Would she herself want to know if Edward were seeing someone else? But the idea was so ludicrous, she couldn't take it seriously.

"Why the sudden interest?" Imogen asked. "Not thinking of divorcing Edward, are you?"

Christina smiled. "No, but if the need arises, I'll be sure to consult you on the finer points of etiquette."

"For the record, Scott and I don't meet if we can help it, either."

"It must be hard on Mia," Christina said reflectively. "And Adam's children too, of course."

"I can't speak for the others, but Mia seems to be adapting better now."

The doorbell heralded another customer, and as Christina went to serve her, Imogen sat back on her heels, surveying her handiwork. But Christina's questions had brought her husband to mind, and with him her own uneasiness.

Something was worrying him, but it seemed he'd no intention of confiding in her. Instead, awake or asleep, he spent the night tossing and turning, muttering and sighing, till she could have screamed. He'd had a couple of restless nights about the time they moved in, she remembered, but since then he'd been fine until a couple of nights ago, when it had all started again. As a result, she was feeling underslept herself and not on top form to start her temporary job, here at French Furnishings. If he was restless again tonight she might consider moving into Mia's room, though she was unsure how he'd react to such a suggestion.

Still, it was the Hardwoods' drinks party this evening; perhaps that would help him to relax. She could only hope so.

"Sonia! I thought it was you!"

Sonia turned from her contemplation of the florist's window to find Eva at her elbow.

"How lovely to see you, dear! I've been meaning to phone, but things have been so hectic since we moved in."

"Hello, Eva." Sonia returned her former mother-in-law's kiss. She was very fond of Eva, but after her traumatic encounter with

Adam, she'd have preferred to avoid anyone connected with him for the moment. Especially Eva, who had always known when something was troubling her.

"Have you time for a coffee?" Eva was continuing. "We can catch up on the news." And without waiting for a reply, she took Sonia's arm and turned with her into the next-door café.

"You weren't on your way to work, were you, dear?" she asked belatedly, as Sonia perforce joined her at the corner table.

"No, Wednesday's my day off."

"That's fine. Are you still at the surgery?"

"Yes, I enjoy it there; and with working only eight thirty to twelve thirty, it gives me time to fit everything else in as well."

Sonia's hesitation in accompanying her had not been lost on Eva, and she was disturbed by it. She'd known Sonia since she was a baby, she and Max having been friendly with her parents, and they'd all been delighted when Adam and Sonia started going out together and later became engaged. Soon after they were married, the Greenwood family, including the newly-weds, moved to London and, missing her own mother, Sonia had frequently turned to Eva for advice. And ironically, all those years later, it had been in Eva's arms that she had sobbed broken-heartedly when her marriage broke down. Which, as Eva admitted to herself, was why she could never really take to Imogen. Comparisons might be odious, but to her mind they were all in Sonia's favour: her air of gentle calm, her smooth cap of chestnut hair and still, grey eyes, as opposed to Imogen's brittle nerviness, her spiky blonde curls and restless, darting glance.

Looking at Sonia now, it struck Eva, not for the first time, that she'd still not got over Adam; and her feelings towards her son, already ambivalent over all this Apostle nonsense, hardened.

"Tell me about the children," she said, when their order had been placed. "I know Adam saw them on Saturday and I'd meant to ask after them, but then all that business with Mia—" She broke off. "Of course, you won't have heard of it." And she told Sonia about the intruder.

"Poor girl," Sonia sympathised, "what a terrifying experience. And what a way for Adam's day out to end. They'd been to Ringmere, then on to the Gables for dinner."

"My goodness, he was pushing the boat out! Tell me, has William gone back yet? I was hoping to see him before he did."

"Yes, he went on Monday, but he comes home now and again for weekends. I know he'd love to see you, and so would the others."

"My fault for not thinking of it sooner, but at least I can see Bethany and Seb. Perhaps you'd like to bring them for lunch on Saturday? At the maisonette, I mean," she added quickly.

Sonia gave a twisted smile. "An Adam-free zone?"

"We keep to our own territories unless invited. Russell and Louise made that rule when we moved in, and I think it's very wise. We don't want to live in each other's pockets, fond as we are of each other."

The coffee arrived, and Eva studied Sonia as she poured it. Something was worrying her; was it just Adam's proximity?

"How are your parents?" she asked. "I had a New Home card from them – I really must give them a ring." It was a relief to Eva that her friendship with the Marshes had survived their children's failed marriage.

"They're well," Sonia replied, wondering how long she could keep up this verbal fencing. "Both as busy as ever; Mum's running the Townswomen's Guild and Dad's become a golf fanatic since he retired. Actually, they were asking if I'd seen you."

There was a brief pause while Sonia toyed with the cake on her plate. Eva said quietly, "Can I help, darling?"

Sonia's eyes flew to her face, and to Eva's consternation, filled with tears. She put her hand quickly over the younger woman's.

"We've always been able to talk, haven't we?" she said gently.

There was a long silence. Perhaps, Eva thought sadly, she had misjudged the situation. Perhaps, despite what she'd believed, they'd grown apart in the years since Sonia had returned to Shillingham.

Then, suddenly, Sonia spoke. "I know it sounds ridiculous, but I'm worried about Adam."

Eva looked at her blankly. She'd guessed Adam was at the root of it, but *worried* about him? "Why is that?"

Sonia drew a deep breath. "I don't know if I should be telling you this, but he didn't say not to."

"You've seen him?" Eva spoke more sharply than she'd intended.

Sonia nodded, and explained about the borrowed pen. "Since William was leaving first thing the next morning, I said I'd drop it in at the studio." Her voice slowed. "Adam arrived there just ahead of me, then I was held up because I had to justify myself to the doorman. I saw the receptionist hand him an envelope, and he took it to the window to open."

She looked up then, meeting Eva's apprehensive eyes. "Eva, I don't know what was in the letter, but he looked ghastly. I thought he was going to pass out. I persuaded him to come home with me and gave him a brandy, then some lunch, and gradually he came round."

"He didn't say what it was about?"

"No, and I didn't ask. Perhaps I should have done."

"And you don't even know who it was from?"

Sonia shook her head. "All I can tell you is that it was hand-delivered and addressed in rather old-fashioned writing to Adam Greenwood, Esquire."

Eva's mouth went dry. The clergyman. It had to be. She moistened her lips. "When was this, Sonia?"

"Monday."

Then he must have been handed it in on Friday afternoon, just before he died. Which perhaps explained his distraction prior to the accident. Oh God, what had Adam got himself into?

Sonia's voice broke into her thoughts. "You know what it was, don't you?"

"I have an idea, that's all. Sonia, if I suddenly said 'the Twelve Apostles', would it mean anything to you?"

She gave a surprised little laugh. "Other than the obvious, not a thing. Why?"

"You wouldn't think of Adam's spoons?"

"His—? Oh, the Apostle spoons. But that's how we always spoke of them – 'the Apostle spoons' – never the Twelve Apostles. I . . ." She stopped, frowning.

Eva leant forward. "What is it?"

Sonia shook her head. "Something stirred vaguely at the back of my mind, but it's gone again. Sorry."

Eva beckoned the waitress. "Well, if you do remember, will you let me know straight away? It might be important."

"Of course, but – why?"

Eva swiftly improvised. "Because we think the intruder might have been after the spoons; Adam had been talking about them on his programme."

"Oh, I see." Sonia looked relieved and Eva suppressed a stab of guilt. But there was no point in worrying the girl, and the fewer people who knew about the Morrison connection, the better.

"You won't let Adam know I mentioned seeing him?"

Eva promised, and having confirmed lunch on Saturday, the two women parted on the pavement outside and went their separate ways, each of them with plenty to think about.

Eva reported the conversation to Verity when she returned home. "It must have been Morrison, mustn't it?" she finished. "There's no other explanation."

"It would explain why he switched to the later train; having failed to talk to Adam after the programme as he'd hoped, he must have decided to put it all down in writing – whatever 'it' was."

Eva said worriedly, "That's the point, isn't it? What could it possibly have been, to have had such a profound effect on Adam?"

"I can't imagine. And I've been thinking about what Mrs Poole said – that her father only wore his dog-collar on official business, as it were. So why was he wearing it when he went to see Adam?"

"We don't know that he was. You didn't notice it at the studio, did you?"

Verity thought back. "No, that's true; I only saw him in profile, and his back view when I followed him to the door. But why bother taking it at all, when he was only going to the hotel and the studio?"

Eva shrugged. "Search me, but I've a nasty feeling that our Mr Morrison poses some kind of threat – though I can't for the life of me think what. Nevertheless, dead or not, I'm pretty sure we haven't heard the last of him."

Webb had spent the day working on reports and papers, but his mind kept returning to the previous day's gruesome findings. Even though locating files would take time, relatives of missing people were already phoning in from all over the country, desperate to know whether the remains could be of their loved one.

Webb had long since overcome his amazement at the number of people who, seemingly every day of the year, went out for cigarettes or to the cinema and were never seen again. At least when a more positive description was available, the calls might diminish. Or would desperate relatives, their memories blurred by the passing years, wishfully meld the features into a semblance of those they had lost? He wished there were a way to reopen such cases without raising false hopes, but if there were, they hadn't discovered it.

And what, he wondered, had happened to all those missing men who *weren't* the owner of these bones? Were they also lying in shallow, unmarked graves? It was a gruesome thought, and Webb pushed it away from him and returned to the work in hand.

*   *   *

In a room on a Cambridge staircase, the occupant was pouring himself a glass of dry sherry when the phone rang.

He reached out to lift it. "Yes?"

"Professor North?"

"Yes?"

"Andrew North, formerly of Broadshire University?"

North frowned. "Yes?" he said, for the third time.

"Greetings, old friend. This is Jeremy Painswick."

There was a pause. Then North said, "Good God! A voice from the past! But I thought—"

"Yes, I know, but something has happened. Did you receive anything unexpected in the post this morning?"

"I left home before it arrived. Why?"

"I imagine there'll be a certain letter waiting for you. When you've read it, call me, will you? If you've a pen handy I'll give you my number."

"You're not at the House?"

"No, it's still the Easter recess."

"Look, Painswick, surely you can give me a hint of—?"

"Not over the phone, old boy. Not wise at all."

"It's surely not to do with—?"

"Phone me when you get home," Painswick repeated, and the line went dead.

Andrew North sat looking at the modest glass of sherry and wished it were a double brandy. *Faute de mieux*, he drained it in one gulp, caught up his briefcase and hurried out of the room.

Imogen was preparing for the Harwoods' party when she heard the phone ring. She hurried to the door but Adam, in the sitting room, had answered it, and she was about to return to her dressing-table when something in the quality of his voice arrested her.

"*Who* did you say? God, what is this – telepathy? I was about to get in touch with you. . . . Yes, yes I did, but I don't think we need worry too much about that. However, there's been a more serious development. . . . No, I agree. . . . I think I could arrange that. Tomorrow? No, I'm sorry, I've got a live programme going out and the day will be spent preparing. Friday, though. . . . I can find it. Yes; eleven thirty, then. Good-bye."

He replaced the phone and stood looking down at it, his hand still resting on the receiver.

"What was that all about?" Imogen asked, appearing in the doorway.

He spun to face her. "How long have you been there? What the hell are you playing at, creeping about like that?"

She stopped dead, the colour flooding up into her face. "Adam!"

"It comes to something if one can't have a private conversation in one's own home! Well, don't just stand there, for God's sake – it's time we were making a move." And before she could collect herself he brushed past her, opened the front door, and strode out on to the forecourt.

Briefly, Imogen closed her eyes, her initial feeling of shock swamped by rising anger. How *dare* he speak to her like that? Who did he think he was?

She drew a deep breath and, catching sight of her flushed cheeks in the mirror, reminded herself that she was about to meet a lot of strangers. She could hardly arrive at someone's house in a towering rage. But Adam's tone had been unpleasantly reminiscent of Scott's in the last, bitter months of their marriage.

Moving slowly and deliberately, she returned to the bedroom, put on the earrings which she'd laid down when the phone rang, and applied a spray of scent. Then she walked out of the flat to where Adam and the others waited by the gate.

Fauconberg House was halfway along Hampton Rise, on the opposite side from Greenwood. It was an imposing house, gracefully proportioned, with Georgian sash windows and a long, immaculately gravelled drive. Two or three cars were parked there, but since this was a neighbourhood party, no doubt most of the guests would come on foot.

Their ring was answered by a uniformed maid, and Elizabeth Harwood came to greet them as they walked into the hall.

"How lovely to see you – do come in. Everyone's looking forward to meeting you."

She led them into the large drawing room, where some dozen people stood talking, glasses in their hands.

"I won't bombard you with names," she said with a smile, "or if you're like me, you'll promptly forget them. My husband you've already met –" she nodded towards Sir Julian, who had not yet caught sight of them – "but let me introduce you to my daughter and son-in-law."

She led them towards a young couple, who turned at their approach. "Mark and Camilla Templeton. Darlings, these are our new neighbours from across the road – the famous Greenwoods! In fact, Adam and Russell might have come across Camilla – she's a television presenter."

"Not peak time, though," Camilla put in, with a charmingly rueful smile. "Afternoons mostly." She was a pretty girl, slim and oval-faced and with her father's deep-set eyes.

"I thought I recognised you!" Louise exclaimed. "I saw that programme you did on gardens a month or two ago."

"And Mark teaches music, both privately and at Ashbourne School."

Louise turned to the tall, serious-looking young man. "You've a struggle ahead with our daughter, I'm afraid – Rebecca Greenwood, she started this term. Musical she isn't!"

"My daughter's been there awhile," Imogen put in, the singular pronoun, though correct, noticeably excluding Adam. "Mia Perry – perhaps you know her?"

"Of course I know Mia – she has a lovely singing voice."

Imogen tried to hide her surprise. Why didn't she know that? They talked for a few minutes, then Elizabeth Harwood led them on to another group, neighbours from farther down the road.

It was amusing, Verity thought, to see how people greeted the two brothers, both of whom were familiar from television. With

116

Russell they were relaxed, asking questions about his travels and congratulating him on his books. Adam, though, provoked a more cautious reaction and was treated with metaphorical kid gloves. Wasn't there an old Scottish proverb – 'Touch not the cat without a glove'?

Verity was watching him herself, aware of tension in the set of his jaw, though he was at his most charming. There was also an atmosphere between him and Imogen, which she hoped wasn't noticeable to the casual observer. She thought again of Eva's conversation with Sonia. What had Mr Morrison written that had so upset Adam? If, of course, the mysterious letter had been from Mr Morrison.

"Mrs Ryder?"

She gave a start and turned to the tall, courteously smiling man who had approached her – her host, Sir Julian.

"I believe you are Naomi Ryder's mother? I'm so sorry – I hadn't made the connection. A very talented young woman; I'm delighted with the bust she's done of me."

"Yes, I saw it," Verity acknowledged. "I thought it was an excellent likeness."

Sir Julian, in fact, looked startlingly like his facsimile; nose, brows and cheeks seemed to have little flesh to cover the underlying bone structure, and his skin was taut and polished. His eyes, a keen, pale blue, were set deep in their sockets, and his fine hair – either fair or grey, it was difficult to tell – thinly covered his scalp from a receding forehead. By narrowing her eyes slightly, it was possible to imagine she was looking at Naomi's bust rather than the living man.

"You'll be coming to the unveiling, of course, at the Arts Centre?"

"Yes, Naomi mentioned it. I believe the date hasn't been fixed yet?"

"Not definitely, no. I also have a date there tomorrow evening, for Adam's programme. *The Development of the Arts over Five Centuries* – quite a large canvas!"

"It certainly is!"

They chatted for several minutes more until everyone was invited to move into the dining room for refreshments. As Sir Julian led her through, Verity noticed Adam automatically take Imogen's elbow, his hand dropping as she quickly moved ahead of him. Oh dear! she thought.

The long table, covered in lace, bore a selection of delectable offerings – smoked salmon, minute quiches, thinly carved meats, vol-au-vents and some half-dozen varieties of salad.

Joined by Eva, Verity took her filled plate back to the drawing room and sat down on a sofa.

"What pleasant neighbours we have," Eva remarked, spearing a stick of asparagus.

"Yes, they all seem very friendly."

"Unlike my eldest son and his wife."

Verity glanced at her. "Yes, I did notice."

"You could cut the atmosphere between them with a knife. Adam's putting on quite a good show, but he's very much on edge. I know the signs."

"If it's still down to that letter," Verity said slowly, "I don't quite see *why* it's thrown him so much. I mean, it sounds an awful thing to say, but the man's dead, isn't he? What harm can he do?"

"Lord knows. I think, you know, I shall have to speak to him – I can't go on like this. On the other hand, I promised Sonia to keep her out of it, which makes it difficult."

"What are you two looking so worried about?" Louise came and perched on a chair beside them. "Isn't the food gorgeous?" she went on, to their relief not waiting for a reply. "We certainly won't need any supper this evening!"

Over her shoulder, Eva saw that Adam had come back into the room, accompanied by an attractive red-haired woman who'd been introduced to her as Mary someone. They were carrying plates of food, and he was smiling attentively as she talked to him. They sat down together across the room, still engaged in

118

conversation. There was no sign of Imogen, and Eva's heart sank.

When they returned to the dining room for dessert, Imogen was sitting with Russell and another couple, also deep in conversation, and as Eva helped herself to some mousse, Imogen's laugh rang out. For whose benefit? she wondered.

Coffee was served afterwards, and it was almost ten by the time the party broke up, with exchanged telephone numbers and promises of future contacts. The April night was cool, and they didn't linger when they reached home, separating to go to their individual front doors.

So now what? Imogen thought, as Adam locked up behind them. Is he going to apologise, or not?

He walked to the drinks table. "Want anything?" he asked, without turning.

"No, thank you."

"After an evening of wine, I need the clean taste of whisky."

"Perhaps it will help you to sleep," she said expressionlessly.

He turned then, his eyes narrowed. "What does that mean?"

"Merely that you've kept me awake for the last two nights, with your tossing and turning."

Adam said nothing, his eyes still on her face as he drank.

It was obvious no apology was forthcoming, either for the disturbed nights or the unwarranted outburst earlier. Imogen took a deep breath.

"In fact, since I need my wits about me at work, I think I'll sleep in Mia's room tonight."

There was a splintered silence. Then Adam said quietly, "Just as you wish," and turned to refill his glass.

Blinded by tears, Imogen went to collect her night things.

Nine

"Dave? Chris Ledbetter here. I thought you might like an update."

"Indeed; how's it going?"

"An interesting development, actually, but God knows if it'll lead anywhere. I've just had Sir Digby Lester on the phone. Ring any bells?"

"Hang on – yes, I think it does. Didn't his son vanish from Broadshire Uni?" His voice quickened. "The time frame would fit, Chris – it must have been soon after I joined the Job."

"Exactly, and the point is this: he wanted to know if we'd dug out his son's file yet. I was explaining about the difficulty in locating it and the time it might take, but he cut me short. Asked if we'd had a dental chart done on the remains, and offered to fax through another copy of his son's. He's getting on to his dentist straight away – seems pretty confident the surgery still has it."

Webb whistled. "Well, that would cut a few corners, not to mention saving any amount of legwork if it proves a match." He thought back. "There was the hell of a hoo-ha at the time. The lad hadn't got his degree, so when he went AWOL the general opinion was that he daren't face his old man. We assumed he'd turn up eventually with his tail between his legs, but he never did."

Webb paused, trying to marry his remembrance of the case with what they'd discovered yesterday.

Ledbetter's voice broke into his reflections. "You're saying he might have topped himself?"

"It was considered possible, when he didn't show up. The whole country was turned upside down, but there was never so much as a whiff of him."

"Well, his father's convinced he's shown up now."

"Poor old boy; fancy living with that uncertainty all these years. The best of luck, Chris. It'll be a real break if this comes off."

Christina said firmly, "Come along, Imogen, we're going for lunch."

Imogen turned from her window-dressing. "But we stagger our lunch hours; I can't—"

"Joseph and Penelope can cope. I want to speak to you."

Imogen tried to smile. "That sounds ominous!"

To her surprise, Christina did not deny it. They crossed East Parade and walked almost in silence down the short street that linked it with Carlton Road, where the Vine Leaf was situated. Imogen was lost in her thoughts, which were not good company. The row with Adam had escalated far beyond what she'd intended, and the night spent apart – which she'd contemplated even before his outburst – seemed to have put the seal on it. She'd slept badly, finally falling into a deep sleep about dawn, and when she woke from it, heavy-eyed and with a headache, it was to discover he'd already left the house.

"So," Christina said, when she'd ordered for both of them, "what's the matter?"

Imogen made a little face. "As obvious as that? I didn't sleep well, that's all, and woke with a bad head. Probably too much wine at the party last night. It'll clear when I've had something to eat."

"Come on, Imo. It's me you're talking to."

Imogen toyed for a moment with the cruet, then looked up, meeting her friend's concerned eyes. "Adam and I had a row," she said flatly. "And – the sun went down on our wrath."

"I see. Was it serious?"

"I don't know. He flared up at me for no reason, and I reacted, that's all."

"Flared up how?"

"Oh, there was some weird phone call when we were getting ready to go out. He arranged to meet whoever it was."

"But you don't know who?"

"No; when I asked him, he blew up – virtually accused me of spying on him – and stormed out of the house."

Christina said quietly, "I could hazard a guess who it might have been."

Imogen stared at her. "What are you talking about?"

"Oh Lord, I didn't want to tell you this, but I think I have to." She paused as two hot goat's cheese salads were laid before them. "You remember I asked if Adam ever saw Sonia?"

"Sonia?" Imogen repeated, clearly bewildered.

"And you said they always tried to avoid each other?"

"Yes?"

"Well, I saw them together, Imo."

Imogen went hot and then cold. "Are you sure? When?"

"Monday morning. Well, about lunchtime, actually. I'd been to collect some material from that wholesaler on Marlton Road, and as I was waiting to cross they drove past."

"Adam and *Sonia*? You're sure it was them?"

"Yes; she was driving. They turned into Sundown Drive."

Imogen moistened her lips. "That's where she lives."

Christina squeezed her hand. "Oh, Imo, I'm so sorry. He – never mentioned seeing her?"

"Of course he didn't bloody mention it." Imogen was close to tears and her temples pounded unbearably. This was much, much worse than she'd thought. She stared miserably at the goat's cheese and her throat closed. There was no way she could eat it. She pushed the plate away from her.

Christina watched her anxiously, already doubting the wisdom of her disclosure. She should have discussed it with Edward first. "It might have been quite innocent," she added belatedly.

123

"When they were going back to her house?" Imogen gave a strangled laugh.

Christina thought a minute, then asked, "Did you gather when this meeting's taking place?"

"Tomorrow; he couldn't manage today because he's tied up with the programme. Oh God, Christy!" Imogen scrabbled for a handkerchief. "I *love* the bastard!" she said, on a furious sob.

Naomi stood at her work table, staring into space. She was now obsessed with the thought that it might have been Nigel who'd broken into the flat, and she couldn't decide whether or not to tell the police. Because, after all, what could she say?

All right, he'd nicked a couple of her things, but in normal circumstances she'd have written that off to experience. Bullying little Mia, however, was another matter. And an appeal *had* been made for information leading to the intruder's arrest.

Well, she thought philosophically, I'm not doing any good here; I can't settle to work with this hanging over me, so I might as well phone them, and have done with it.

Before she changed her mind again, she went through to the living room, looked up the number of the police station, and dialled it.

"I'm ringing about the attempted burglary last Saturday," she said. "The one in Hampton Rise, when the young girl was held."

There was a pause while she was connected with an officer dealing with the case and, by now regretting having contacted them, she outlined what to her ears sounded very feeble reasons for her suspicions.

The police, however, seemed to think differently. To her surprise, she was told they'd like to come round and examine the flat for finger and shoe prints, fibres and so on, which might match those taken from the scene. And even as she was contemplating doing a quick tidy, the officer added, "I realise you must have dusted and swept since he left, madam, but could I ask you to leave everything as it is now, until we get there?"

And Naomi, who had put off her intended cleaning and had in fact neither dusted nor swept since Saturday, magnaminously agreed.

It was four thirty when Webb's phone rang again and Ledbetter's jubilant voice said in his ear, "Bingo! The remains are confirmed as those of Piers Lester, aged twenty-two at the time he went missing. The fax is an exact match, and a certified copy's on its way."

"Hallelujah!" Webb exclaimed. "Now all we have to do is find out how he died and who buried him."

"That's right, put a dampener on it!"

"Sorry! At least we're well ahead of where we expected to be."

"All the same, you were right; now the ID's established, it's virtually back to square one. I've been looking at Lester's file – it was given priority after the phone call – and there were certainly plenty of people interviewed at the time. God knows how many of them we'll be able to locate. Still, let's look on the bright side; we're over the first hurdle, and who knows, perhaps our luck will hold."

"Lou? I've a favour to ask."

"Hi, Naomi. Of course, fire away."

"Could I scrounge a bed for tonight? I have to be out of my flat."

"How do you mean, out? You've not been evicted, have you?"

Naomi laughed. "Hardly, I own the place. The thing is, though, I don't want to sound cloak-and-dagger about this but I'd rather no one else knew about it. Not Adam and Imogen, and not Mother or Eva, either."

"That *does* sound mysterious. Can you tell me why?"

"The police are here."

Louise said incredulously, "Don't tell me *you've* had a break-in?"

"No, it's to do with my ex-lodger, but I'll explain when I see you. You're sure it won't put you out?"

"Of course not. Come for dinner – we were going to arrange a meal anyway. Then you can tell us all about it."

"I thought you'd be going to Adam's programme?"

"No, we passed this time. We're hoping to go to the school next week, though – that should be interesting, and we'll be able to see Mia."

"How is she, I've been meaning to ask? Was she very upset by what happened?"

"Oddly enough, no. I thought she'd retreat still further into her shell, but she's perkier than I've ever seen her." There was a smile in Louise's voice. "Tom's rather smitten, and I think his attentions took her mind off it."

"Tom? Ye gods, it seems no time since he was in a Babygro! Doesn't it make you feel old?"

"Positively ancient! Anyway, I'll make up the spare bed and swear Russell to secrecy. The children will have to know, though."

"I'm sure they'll be discreet. Thanks, Louise. About six?"

"Fine. See you then."

Over dinner, therefore, Naomi explained about Nigel's abrupt departure on the day in question and his apparent interest in the value of the spoons.

"He's pinched things from me, so he's not squeaky clean," she finished. "All the same, I might well be wronging him in this instance – in fact, I probably am. But if by any chance it *was* Nigel, then at least the police will have a lead. And if it wasn't, there'll be no harm done."

"So they're searching for his fingerprints in your flat?" Rebecca was wide-eyed.

"I don't see how they could help," Russell commented, "since the police have nothing to compare them with; they didn't find any at Adam's."

"It's more fibres they're interested in, and hairs and minuscule things like that. Apparently we shed them all over the place –

charming thought, isn't it? They removed several from Mia's coat and skirt which they think were transferred from her attacker."

"If he *is* her attacker, he deserves all he gets," Tom said in a low voice.

"Exactly. Now, enough of all that; how are you two liking your new schools? Or is it too early to say?"

"I have only been there one day," Tom pointed out. "Seems OK, though. What I *don't* enjoy is having to get up so early."

"To catch the commuters' express to Broadminster," Russell explained. "Actually, it's very convenient; the bus stop's within fifty yards, on the corner of Hunter's Hill, and as buses meet all the Broadminster trains, he's dropped off again virtually at the gate. You've got it cushy, my boy. At your age, I had a three-mile bike ride to school."

"Not as cushy as Rebecca," Tom objected humorously. "She only has to walk down the hill – seven minutes, door to door. I reckon that over the term she'll have several hours' more sleep than I will!"

"You could board if you wanted to," his father told him, but Tom smilingly shook his head.

"And what of the famous Ashbourne?" Naomi asked Rebecca.

"That's OK, too. Everyone's excited about the programme next week. Mia says she's teased about Uncle Adam being rude to everyone, but they can't wait to see him in person."

Louise glanced at her watch. "We must keep an eye on the time; it's eight o'clock already, so if you two have any homework to do, I suggest you go and do it now. Then you can come downstairs to watch the programme. If you want to, that is."

Tom shrugged. "Might as well, since we've a project looming on the quincentenary. Personally, though, I prefer Uncle's usual programmes, when you never know what might happen."

"I doubt if your grandmother would agree with you!" Russell said with a smile.

* * *

Imogen, too, was watching the time. Since Christina's bombshell at lunch, she had been going over and over in her mind all the conversations she'd had with Adam since their arrival here.

When had this thing with Sonia started? She'd not been at the studio last week, but that was the evening Imogen first noticed something was troubling him. During the programme itself he'd been relaxed and in good spirits, yet that night his lovemaking had had a desperate edge to it – and what was it he'd said afterwards? "We have a good life together, don't we? You do love me?"

Hardly the words of a straying husband.

Since then, what with the break-in, and Elliott and Maggie coming, and Adam out all day planning his programme, and herself working, they'd had little time to talk to each other, but his restless nights were further indication of a troubled mind.

And so to the phone call last night. *Had* it been Sonia on the line, as Christina suggested? It seemed foolhardly for her to risk phoning the flat. Yet even if it hadn't been, the fact that she and Adam had been seen together going in the direction of her house could not be gainsaid. Perhaps, Imogen thought miserably, he'd been with her at other times, too, when she thought he was working.

She pressed the remote control. The nine o'clock news was just finishing, but faces and places passed before her eyes without her registering them. A picture of woods and a country lane caught her attention, with blue and white police tape closing off the path, but she'd missed the beginning of the item and its significance was lost on her. The weather forecast followed, and at last the familiar music and titles on the screen: *Adam Greenwood Live – in Shillingham.*

The opening shot was of the Arts Complex, an imposing building in the centre of town. Adam, recorded earlier in the day, stood outside it, describing its history and the breadth of services it offered. Then, the introduction over, the camera moved inside to the concert hall, the audience started applauding, and Adam walked on to the platform.

Was Sonia in the audience? Imogen wondered. Had she, perhaps, received a special invitation? And suppose, after Imogen's seeming rejection of him last night, Adam went back with her after the programme? Had she, by her display of hurt pride, only thrown them closer together?

Sir Julian Harwood had appeared, and was speaking interestingly about the development of music, while pictures of ancient instruments flashed on the screen. Imogen only half-listened, too unhappy to concentrate, greedy for every glimpse of Adam as the camera panned from one speaker to the other, searching for any sign of the unrest within him. But Adam, at home in front of the camera, had long since learned to conceal his thoughts and she could detect nothing.

His second guest, though, did hold Imogen's attention; introduced as Mary Derringer, the well-known historian, she proved to be none other than the red-haired woman from last night's party. Was this all they'd been talking about so animatedly over supper? Imogen felt she was becoming paranoid.

Miss Derringer was an excellent speaker, and, under Adam's astute questioning, what she had to say about drama, art and literature over the centuries was absorbing. Mention of strolling players and of Mystery plays performed from wagons set up on the Broadminster road made Imogen see her home town with new eyes, and she determined to find out more about its history.

When the programme ended, however, the spell was broken, her worries came flooding back, and she knew despairingly that she'd have no peace until she'd asked Adam about Sonia, even if it widened the gulf between them still further.

Eventually, after what seemed an agonising wait, she heard his key in the door and a minute later he came into the room. He looked totally exhausted and she felt her resolution falter.

"Hello," he said. "Catch the programme?"

She nodded and he gave a twisted smile. "No need to rave about it!"

"It was very interesting," she said. Then, before her courage failed completely, added quickly, "Adam, I know you've been seeing Sonia."

He stared at her. "I've *what*?"

"Don't pretend, because I shan't believe you. You were seen together."

"May I ask when, and by whom?"

"Monday," she said, ignoring the second part of the question.

"Ah."

" 'Ah'?" she repeated, her voice rising. "Is that all you can say?"

"You don't seem to have a very high opinion of me, Imogen."

How dared he turn the blame on her? "What else am I to think, when you're seen driving to her home? Especially as you never mentioned seeing her."

Without a word he went to the drinks table, poured two stiff whiskies and handed her one. She took it. "Well?"

"You can tell your informer it was all quite innocent. I was – taken ill at the studio, and she kindly took me back with her till I'd recovered."

"You didn't tell me you'd been ill."

"It was nothing much – it soon passed."

"And she just *happened* to be there?"

"Actually, yes. She was returning my pen, which I'd lent William the day before."

Imogen gazed at him, reassembling the facts into a far less threatening pattern. Oh God, what had she done, accusing him of heaven knew what, when—?

"Well? Do you believe me or not?"

"Of course I believe you," she said in a low voice.

"Are you really so insecure as to imagine I'd go back to Sonia?"

She shook her head wordlessly, not meeting his eyes. He took the glass out of her hand and put it, together with his own, on a low table. Then he gently pulled her to her feet and put his arms round her, his face on her hair.

"Don't you desert me, Imogen," he said. "I need at least someone on my side."

"I'm sorry," she whispered and raised her head, expecting him to kiss her as a prelude to their usual post-programme love-making. But this evening he seemed to have other things on his mind, for after a moment, with a little pat, he put her away from him and turned to the television.

"I want to see the late-night headlines," he said, switching it on. And there again was the picture she'd seen earlier, of the wood and the police tape, and this time she made the connection with the recent discovery of bones.

"Broadshire police have today confirmed that the remains found in Fox Woods earlier this week are those of the university student Piers Lester, only son of financier Sir Digby Lester, who disappeared without trace in 1972. The investigation has been reopened and police will re-question previous witnesses in an effort to determine how Mr Lester met his death."

Adam pressed the button and the screen went blank. He remained staring at it, his reflection now mirrored where his image had been an hour earlier.

Imogen moved towards him, put her hand on his arm. "Darling?"

"I knew him," he said, "Piers Lester. We were up together."

"Oh, Adam, I'm so sorry!" Memory stirred. "And didn't another university friend die recently? You were reading about it the day we moved in."

"Dropping like flies," Adam said expressionlessly. "Except that it seems Piers 'dropped' nearly thirty years ago."

He turned away abruptly, pulling off his tie. "Bedtime," he said. Then he stopped, turning to look back at her. "Are you retiring to your chaste couch again?"

"No."

"Even though my tossing and turning might disturb you?"

"I'll risk it."

He smiled then, and reached out a hand to her. She came forward to take it and, switching off the lights behind them, they went to their room.

Sonia had also watched the programme, with Bethany and Seb, and like Imogen had scoured Adam's face for signs of the strain that had been so blatant on Monday. There were none that she could see; did that mean he was himself again?

Her mind went back, as it had countless times, to the hour or so they'd spent together. What could possibly have been in that letter? she wondered yet again. And how much did Eva know, or guess, about the sender?

Eva herself was at that moment sitting up in bed, her book unread on her lap. Beyond the circle of the lamplight the room lay in shadow, its layout already familiar and comforting. Her eyes moved over it – the elegant curtains at the window, the button-back chair on which she had nursed her children, the thick, luxurious carpet. It was exactly as she'd hoped it would be, and she knew without doubt that this had been a wise move. All that marred her complete contentment was her worry over Adam.

Sonia's story about the letter and its traumatic effect on him had resurrected all her fears, convincing her that he had indeed known that clergyman. So why had he lied?

The Twelve Apostles. They kept cropping up. Not only in Morrison's dying words, but in Elliott's comments last Sunday. What had he said? "Adam's always been obsessed by the Twelve Apostles." Like Verity, she had caught – and been puzzled by – the exchange of glances between her elder sons.

She frowned as something stirred at the back of her mind, something concerning her talk with Sonia. When Eva had asked if the words meant anything to her, and Sonia'd said no, she'd explained that she and Adam always spoke of 'the Apostle spoons', not of 'the Twelve Apostles'.

Exactly! Eva thought, sitting up straighter. So did they all – so had Adam during the interview. Surely, then, if Mr Morrison had been referring back to the programme, he also would have said, 'The Apostle spoons', rather than 'The Twelve Apostles'? She remembered uneasily that it was Adam who'd suggested the spoon connection, and the rest of them had accepted it.

But if Morrison *hadn't* meant the spoons, what could he have meant? And Elliott too, for that matter? Was there some other implication?

Eva lay back against her pillows, thinking deeply. It was not as though Adam collected anything else to do with the Apostles – religious artefacts or ornaments or paintings.

She pushed back the bedclothes, padded over to the chest-of-drawers where she had replaced her own set of spoons after showing them to Verity, and took them back to bed. Then she opened the box and stared down at the small figures, each with his symbol. Never in all the years she'd had them had she paid them as much attention as she had over the last week.

What secret were they hiding? Why did they seem to be threatening Adam?

Eva shook herself. She was becoming fanciful. She closed the box, fastened the tiny gold catch, and set it down on the bedside table. Then with a sigh – because, after all, she had not solved anything – she switched off the lamp and settled down to sleep.

Ten

The following morning Imogen viewed Christina with mixed feelings. No doubt she'd meant well, reporting her sighting of Adam and Sonia, but it had caused Imogen a great deal of heartache and could have precipitated a full-scale row with Adam. Thankfully, that had not happened.

Christina, catching her eye, came across. "All right?"

"More than all right. It was a false alarm."

Christina's eyebrows rose.

"Adam wasn't well, that's all, and Sonia came to his rescue." Aware of her friend's scepticism, she added a little impatiently, "Honestly, Christy, there was nothing in it, believe me."

Christina put a hand on her arm. "That's great, Imo. I couldn't be more pleased. I'm so sorry I worried you unnecessarily."

She returned to her work, mentally upbraiding herself. Last night, when she'd told Edward what she'd done, he'd been critical. "No one ever thanks you for passing on something like that. In such cases, darling, silence is golden. Remember that."

And she would, Christina told herself fervently. All the same, she couldn't help wondering if Imogen had found out who'd made that mysterious phone call.

In fact, Imogen had not. Adam had merely told her he'd be spending the day in London, and the recently restored equanimity between them was too precious to risk any probing. The important thing was that peace had been restored.

*   *   *

135

"Spider?"

Webb sighed and tucked the phone under his chin. "Good-morning, sir."

"Spoken to Ledbetter this morning?"

"Not yet; there's a message to call him on my desk."

"It's about that list of people interviewed in the Lester case. We've been landed with a hornets' nest, I can tell you. Several of them are now household names – including that chap Green-wood, who's on the box."

Webb straightened. "Adam or Russell?"

"The one who's spouting off about Shillingham. Adam, isn't it? He was up there at the time, along with these other chaps. We've got the lot here – writers, bankers, MPs, professors – even that film director, Van whatever his name is."

"Van Hoek," Webb supplied, "Chester Van Hoek."

"That's the one. Yank, of course."

"Sounds as though we've an interesting time ahead of us, sir."

"Yes. Point is this, Spider. These types need careful handling; probably wouldn't take kindly to being grilled by a DC, or whatever."

Webb raised an eyebrow, surprised that the old man should bow to celebrity status. In his book, there was no reason why a DC shouldn't 'grill' the highest in the land, if the case so warranted. He knew what was coming, though, and sure enough it came.

"So I'd like you to take on some of them personally. I've arranged with Ledbetter to have their files sent over."

Webb held back a sigh. "Have we anything new to go on, sir?" From what he remembered of the case, it had been exhaustively investigated at the time.

"What's new," Fleming replied waspishly, "is that we now know the fellow was dead all along – dead and buried. I shouldn't have to remind you of that, Superintendent."

"No, sir."

"Like it or not, Spider – and personally I don't – we've got a high-profile case on our hands, not only with the victim's father but those who were around at the time. The media will be following our every move on this. I know I can rely on your discretion."

The town of Steeple Bayliss had grown up on the north side of a chasm carved out by the last Ice Age. A sheer cliff face rose steeply from the banks of the River Darrant, and at its foot some half-dozen cottages nestled into the hillside.

The south side had remained uncultivated until the nineteenth century, when it was chosen as the site of Broadshire University, whose grounds sloped more gently down to the river. The chasm itself was spanned by a viaduct, from where there was a magnificent view of the river far below, with its gently rocking boats and the permanently moored Barley Mow, a converted grain barge which was now a public house.

DI Ledbetter and his sergeant, however, didn't spare it a glance, their minds on the interview ahead. Leaving the main road, they turned into the university entrance, a long driveway which wound through rows of trees, with frequent lead-offs to different halls of residence. Eventually the avenue opened into a large space like the centre of a village, surrounded by imposing-looking buildings of honey-coloured stone.

The students had returned from their Easter break, and as the two detectives got out of their car, groups of them hurried past carrying satchels and armfuls of books, on their way to the main faculty buildings. The two men followed more slowly, preparing to beard the lion in his den.

Their appointment was with Sir Humphrey Nichols, the Senior Deputy Chancellor, a tall, well-built man in his late fifties, and he greeted them pleasantly enough.

"Sit down, gentlemen, sit down." He indicated a file on his desk. "When I heard you were coming, I had the papers on the incident sent up from the archives and I've been rereading them. They bring it all back – I was a tutor here at the time – and I'm more than sorry that our worst fears have been realised. However, as these papers remind me, the police lost no time in setting up extensive enquiries, and for the life of me I can't see how I or my staff can help you at this late stage."

Nor could Ledbetter. "Perhaps, sir, you wouldn't mind telling us what you remember, both about Mr Lester and his disappearance."

Sir Humphrey pursed his lips. "Well, I've no wish to speak ill of the dead, but Piers Lester wasn't one of our more illustrious students. In fact, he did as little work as he could get away with, and it was no surprise that he failed his finals. Nor, from what I gleaned, was he particularly popular with his fellows."

He paused, surveying them under bushy eyebrows. "Naturally, I shouldn't wish this to get back to his father."

Ledbetter assured him it was confidential.

"As to the actual disappearance," Sir Humphrey continued, "it remains a mystery. It was the end of the academic year, exams were over, and the students were somewhat – exuberant, as they tend to be. On the night in question, at least half a dozen parties were being held on campus, and others in houses around the town. Lester could have been at any or none of them. There are no reports of his having being seen at all that evening; as far as I remember, the last sighting of him was around four o'clock, having tea in the refectory."

"By himself?" Ledbetter asked, thinking it was no wonder the inquiry had led nowhere.

Sir Humphrey nodded.

"Was he in one of the halls of residence, sir?"

"No, they're mainly for first-year students. He had lodgings – I have the address somewhere." He shuffled through the papers on his desk.

"Here we are, with a Mrs Freebody at number twelve Farthing Lane. God knows if she's still there, but it seems she couldn't help much at the time."

"Had she other students there as well?"

"No, just him. Most of them get together and rent houses in the final year."

But no one had invited Piers to join them. Ledbetter began to feel sorry for the boy.

"Were any of his things missing from the lodgings?"

"Not that the woman could tell. His suitcases were still there, and his clothes."

"So it didn't look as though he'd planned his departure?"

"No. There was some conjecture that he took off on the spur of the moment, but that's hardly feasible. In any case, he was at liberty to leave if he wanted to; quite a few of the students had already gone home."

"Did he have a car?"

"He'd pranged it a week earlier. It was in the garage for repairs."

Another lost lead. Ledbetter tried again. "Was there anyone he was on particularly bad terms with?"

"I'm afraid I can't help you there, Inspector; I wasn't one of his tutors."

"Is there anyone still here who was?"

"There's Graham Pemberton. Excellent chap – he's a Reader now. If you like, I'll ask my secretary to ring through and see if he's free."

Minutes later, they were informed that Mr Pemberton was indeed free, and willing to see them. Ledbetter thanked Sir Humphrey, nodded to Hopkins, and rose to his feet. They'd not learned anything new; in all probability the inquiry was doomed to failure, as it had been first time round. Still, they'd have a word with Pemberton and the landlady, and see what they had to say.

Graham Pemberton was a bluff, hearty man, almost completely bald and a couple of stone overweight.

"It was a shock," he admitted, "when those bones were identified. I didn't particularly like Piers, but he was still one of my students."

"Anything you can tell us about him, sir, would be most useful."

"He was an odd kind of guy," Pemberton said reflectively. "I was his personal tutor, but I never discovered what made him tick."

"Bit withdrawn, was he? Kept himself to himself?"

Pemberton gave a snort. "Far from it – he was always trying to push in where he wasn't wanted. Too much to say, too. You know the type – constant repartee and clever remarks. It can be very wearing, but he couldn't seem to see he got everyone's back up."

"Everyone's? Including yours, sir?"

Pemberton looked slightly abashed. "I admit I lost my rag with him once or twice, but it was water off a duck's back. I'd started off being sorry for the lad, but it soon became clear he either didn't see or wouldn't admit there was any problem. At any rate, he rejected all my attempts to help him."

"What about girlfriends?"

Pemberton shrugged. "There were a few, but they never lasted long. To give the devil his due, he was a good-looking chap – fair hair, blue eyes." Pemberton's own eyes flicked to the handsome inspector, and away again. "Now you mention it, though, there was one girl who caused a rumpus – complained he'd come on too strong, if you understand me. Added to which, she was going with someone else at the time."

"Who would that have been, sir? Her regular boyfriend, I mean?"

"Now you're asking." Pemberton leant back and gazed up at the ceiling. "One of the gang, if I remember aright. Who was it, now?"

"The gang?"

"A misnomer, Inspector – just my personal name for them. A group of clever young men who went around together. Done well for themselves since, too, from what I've heard."

Probably on Dave Webb's list, then, Ledbetter thought. "Who was in this 'gang', sir?"

140

"Oh, Matthew Henderson, the best-seller writer, Jeremy Painswick, Adam Greenwood – there was quite a crowd of them."

"And Mr Lester pinched one of their girlfriends?" It hardly seemed likely.

"I heard that someone dared her to go out with him. He, naturally, thought she fancied him, and tried it on. You could hardly blame him. But the stupid woman became hysterical and the fur flew. A storm in a teacup, if you ask me."

"It would help," Ledbetter said carefully, "if you could remember some names."

"I'm trying, Inspector, I'm trying. Carla – that was the girl. Carla Keating. Legs up to her armpits. And the chap was . . . Felix Lytton. Yes, that's right."

"The newspaper magnate?" Ledbetter asked incredulously.

Pemberton smiled. "The very same. I told you they'd done well."

"And when you say the fur flew, what exactly happened?"

"Oh, just a bout of fisticuffs. Piers measured his length on the floor, but later he was heard boasting about it in the bar."

"How long was this before Lester's disappearance?"

Pemberton shrugged. "A week or two. But it was no big deal, Inspector; when Felix heard Carla'd gone with Piers for a bet, he broke off with her anyway."

"And blamed Mr Lester?"

"No, he was too fair-minded for that."

So what had seemed a promising lead had fizzled out before it really got going. No doubt this was all in Lytton's file anyway. All they could do was thank Pemberton for his help and hope for more luck with the landlady.

Farthing Lane was a narrow road behind the High Street, and parking was at a premium. The detectives therefore left their car at the police station and set off on foot for the ten-minute walk. At least it was a lovely spring morning.

"Glorious day, isn't it?" Ledbetter commented, and Hopkins grunted in reply. Ledbetter flicked a sideways glance at his lugubrious face and smiled inwardly. Not for nothing was Hopkins ironically known at the station as 'Happy'.

The High Street was thronged with shoppers, young women in the summer dresses that always came out with the first burst of sunshine, often prematurely. There was still a cool breeze, and personally Ledbetter was glad of his winter-weight jacket.

Farthing Lane, screened from the sun by the tall buildings of the High Street, was even cooler, and the men shivered as they stood on the doorstep of number twelve.

"She's probably out," Hopkins said morosely, but even as he spoke they heard footsteps approaching from the inside, and a stout, pleasant-faced woman stood looking at them enquiringly.

"Mrs Freebody? DI Ledbetter and DS Hopkins." They held up their warrant cards. "Do you think we could have a word?"

"You've come about Piers, I suppose," she said, her face clouding. "I never stopped hoping that he'd turn up somewhere, safe and sound."

She moved aside to let them in, and Ledbetter registered that this was the first positive thing anyone had said about the dead man.

"You got on well with him?" he asked, as they settled themselves in the small front room.

"Like a son, he was. Never had one of my own, just three daughters, though I wouldn't be changing any of them, mind. He'd such a sense of humour, too – kept me and my husband in stitches."

Someone had appreciated him, then. Ledbetter was glad.

"Can you tell us anything about the day he disappeared? Did he seem upset at all?"

"Not a bit of it. Looking forward to going home at the end of the week, though he did say he'd miss his friends."

"Friends?"

"Oh, he was very popular, was Piers, up at the university. Always telling us about those pals of his and what they all got up to."

Ledbetter digested that in silence. "So when he left the house for the last time," he said after a moment, "there was nothing to indicate he wouldn't be coming back?"

"Nothing at all. He'd had invites to several parties so we knew he'd be late home, but he had a key so I thought nothing of it. Only discovered in the morning that his bed hadn't been slept in. Even then we didn't worry, knowing what young people are. But when there was no word from him that day nor the next neither, then George said we should tell the police."

"No one from the university tried to contact him?"

"No. I thought that was funny at first, with him knowing so many people. You'd think someone would have missed him. But it was the end of term and they were all coming and going and I suppose they lost track of each other. When I think, though, of him lying out there all alone all these years—" Her voice broke and she reached into her skirt pocket for a handkerchief.

Ledbetter gave her a moment to recover, then asked, "Did he mention any friends in particular?"

"Oh, there were so many I can't remember them now. Fancy names for the most part, but you'd expect that, wouldn't you? I mean, 'Piers' isn't your usual run, is it?"

Ledbetter agreed that it wasn't. "Felix?" he hazarded.

"Yes!" Mrs Freebody confirmed eagerly. "That was one. I used to think it sounded more like a cat!"

"What about girls?"

"Oh, he was never short of them! There was one in particular, though, he talked a lot about. Carla – there, it's coming back to me now. But she was too keen, and in the end he had to finish with her. 'Sometimes, Mrs F, you have to be cruel to be kind,' he said. Such a nice young man."

It seemed to be the best epitaph Piers Lester could hope for, and Ledbetter let it stand. Thanking Mrs Freebody for her time, he and Hopkins took their leave.

Later that day, he phoned Webb to pass on the information he had gained.

"Yep, Felix Lytton's on my list," Webb confirmed. "I'm having the devil of a job tracking them all down, though. Each one I tried, I was told 'Mr So-and-So's out for lunch and won't be back for the rest of the day.' Some lunches they have, these tycoons! No wonder the country's in a parlous state. Even Adam Greenwood's off to London for the day."

As Webb put down the phone a few minutes later, there was a knock on his door and DC Barbara Day put her head round it. "Can you spare a minute, Guv?"

"Of course, Babs, come in."

She perched on the chair in front of his desk. "I thought you could do with a bit of good news, so I've brought you some."

"Praise be! What is it?"

"Remember the woman who phoned in about her lodger, and SOCO went round to her flat?"

"I heard about it, yes."

"She thought he might have been the one who broke into Greenwood that night. Well, she was right!"

"You've not found him already?"

"The Met has. We circulated his name and description, really expecting he'd be using an alias, but not a bit of it. He simply went home to his basement flat, bold as brass, and was there when the Met went knocking on his door. They recovered some things he'd stolen from Miss Ryder, which were lying quite openly on a table, and the fibres of his jacket matched those taken from the flat and the girl's clothes."

"As easy as that," Webb commented. "Well, it restores your faith, I suppose."

"The odd thing is," Barbara Day continued, "the woman in

question is the sister of the girl's aunt – or step-aunt, if there is such a thing."

"You've lost me!"

She smiled. "Naomi Ryder is the sister of Louise Greenwood, sister-in-law of Adam Greenwood, who is the girl's stepfather."

Webb put his head in his hands. "I think it was clearer the first time!"

"Funny, though, isn't it? That she should have a lodger like that, I mean. When she phoned in she said he'd pinched things from her in the past, but he hasn't got a record."

"An opportunist rather than a professional, then."

"Believe it or not, he calls himself a poet."

"Let's hope he's got a rhyme for burglary. Well done, Babs. Has anyone informed Miss Ryder and the Greenwoods he's been caught?"

"I'll check, sir."

Webb nodded and resumed his work.

Hannah had just returned to her flat that afternoon when the phone rang.

"Hannah?" The voice was male, high-pitched and breathless-sounding.

"Yes?"

"It's Nicholas. Nicholas King."

Hannah was surprised; Nicholas King, an accomplished concert pianist, was married to her friend Pamela and had on occasion given performances at Ashbourne. But they were not on telephoning terms, and she felt a clutch of apprehension.

"Hello, Nicholas; how's Pamela?"

"She's fine." Hannah breathed a sigh of relief. "However," he went on a little jerkily, "it's because you're her friend that I'm phoning."

It sounded ominous. Hannah sat down, and the marmalade cat which had been circling her legs jumped up on her knee. "Yes?"

145

"There's something urgent I need to discuss with you – not over the phone, though. I'm down at the cottage."

The Kings lived in Wimbledon but had a country home at Chipping Claydon, a village some ten miles from Shillingham.

Hannah frowned. "Is Pamela with you?"

"No."

"Does she know you're phoning me?"

"No. I'll explain later. The point it, could you come out and see me?"

Hannah's eyebrows went up. "It would be more convenient if you came to Shillingham," she said a little stiffly.

"Humour me, Hannah, please. It's important."

Some quality in his voice deepened her unease. "You're not ill, are you?" she asked sharply. Heaven forbid he wanted her to tell his wife he was dying.

"No, not ill, but I do need to see you urgently."

"I suppose I could come tomorrow," she said reluctantly, stroking the cat's ears.

"Tomorrow?" he repeated impatiently. "What's wrong with this evening?"

"I have a dinner engagement."

"Surely you could break it?"

"No," Hannah answered steadily, aware of rising anger, "I couldn't." She remembered now that Pamela was always expected to run round after him. Well, she had no intention of doing so.

There was another pause. "All right," he conceded at last, "tomorrow it will have to be. But as soon as you can make it, please. I'll see you then." And he rang off.

Hannah slammed the phone down, admitting to herself that she'd never really liked the man. Tall and thin with a slight stoop, he seemed to be a bag of nerves and was constantly twitching and fidgeting. She'd suffered him for Pamela's sake and because of his undoubted talent, but wondered how her friend managed to live with him.

Tipping the cat on to the floor, Hannah went through to the kitchen, accompanied by its loud purring. As she opened the tin of cat food, she thought suddenly of the joke about the man who fell for the voice of an ageing opera star; on the morning after the wedding he took one look at her and exclaimed, "For God's sake, sing!" Perhaps Pamela felt the same.

Smiling to herself, Hannah bent down to feed the cat.

The dinner appointment she had mentioned was, in fact, at David's. It had been arranged before the Lester case surfaced, but a quick phone call this morning had confirmed that he still expected her.

David had taught himself to cook years before when his wife left him, determined not to live out of tins like so many of his bachelor colleagues. Now he was most proficient, enjoying the challenge of sophisticated cuisine as a relaxation when pressure of work weighed him down. Hannah teased him that the more complicated a case became, the more elaborate his cooking.

While she showered and changed, her thoughts circled round Nicholas King and his curious request; and the more she thought about it, the less she felt like complying. Why should she make a round trip of twenty miles, when the man was perfectly capable of meeting her here?

Yet there'd been something in his manner which prevented her from simply resolving not to go. That he was worried was obvious; but if he couldn't confide in his wife, who better than her twin sister, who also lived in Broadshire? Surely Paula would have been the obvious confidante.

It was as she slipped on her dress that Hannah hit on the perfect solution: she'd ask David to go with her.

Half an hour later, therefore, as they sat over their drinks before dinner, she broached the subject.

"Do you remember my speaking of Paula Welling? I cat-sat for her in Honeyford that summer."

"And became involved in two particularly nasty murders,"

Webb finished drily. "How could I forget? Though I never met the lady."

"She and her twin sister, Pamela, were at Ashbourne with me and we've remained friends. Paula's still single, but Pamela married Nicholas King and went to live in Wimbledon. They have a weekend cottage in Chipping Claydon."

Webb stretched out his long legs and regarded her quizzically. "And exactly what is all this leading up to?"

"Well, I had a very strange phone call from Nicholas this evening, asking me to go out to the cottage to meet him. Pamela isn't there, apparently."

"Ah-hah!"

"He says he wants to discuss something urgent, but wouldn't say what. In fact, he asked me to break our dinner date and go this evening."

"Did he, indeed?"

"I suggested he came over here tomorrow, but he insists that I go there. Lord knows why. He was so edgy that in the end I said I'd drive out in the morning." She hesitated. "I'm probably being silly, but – I wondered if you'd come with me?"

Webb raised an eyebrow. "Officially, or simply as moral support?"

"I'm not sure. The latter, I suppose."

"But if an old friend wants to speak to you urgently, he's not going to be too pleased if you turn up with another bloke he's never set eyes on."

"I wouldn't describe Nicholas as an old friend. Anyway, you could wait in the car. To be honest, I don't fancy being alone with him in some deserted cottage, especially when he's in this strange mood."

"I'm sorry, love; normally, I'd be only too happy to oblige, but I've got the Chief Super on my back and I really have to catch up with some of these—" He broke off. "What did you say this bloke's name is?"

"Nicholas King."

"The concert pianist?"

"Yes. David, what is it?"

"I think your luck might be in – he's one of the people on my list. It didn't click before; I'd mentally switched off from work, and hearing the name in a different context didn't ring a bell."

"But I don't understand; why do you have to see him?"

"Because, my love, he was at uni with the late, lamented Piers Lester, and I want him to help me with my enquiries."

"Perhaps that's what's worrying him," said Hannah.

Eleven

Tony Poole came into the kitchen as his wife was preparing breakfast.

"I'm going to the library this morning," he said, "so I'll take this book of Pop's back."

Catherine glanced at the detective novel with a rueful smile. "He was really enjoying it, bless him; now he'll never know who dunnit."

"On the contrary," Tony said, "he'll have all the answers." He sat down at the table, flicking the book open. "His bookmark's still in it," he added, removing a slip of paper. Idly, he unfolded it, and frowned.

"That's odd; it's a list of names and addresses."

Catherine moved across and looked over his shoulder. The list had been painstakingly typed on her father's old manual, and the names on it were familiar. "Apart from the first one, those were the people I posted letters to," she said.

"They're a pretty eminent lot," her husband commented. "Just look at them – authors, musicians, even a film director, for heaven's sake. Do you think Pop was a closet fan?"

"Hardly, and some are more down to earth; there's a couple of professors and an MP."

"Adam Greenwood; wasn't that the man whose TV show he went to?" The Pooles were not avid viewers and Adam's notoriety had passed them by.

"Hang on a minute." Tony looked up at his wife. "That woman with Mrs Ryder, who joined us for coffee: wasn't her name Greenwood?"

151

"Yes," Catherine said slowly, "I think it was. How strange. Do you think she was any relation?"

"Well, it's not all that common a name. But when we mentioned there was a ticket to the show in Pop's wallet, surely she'd have said something? It would have been only natural."

"I'm not so sure," Catherine said consideringly. "We were all a bit subdued after the inquest, remember; perhaps she thought it would sound like bragging if she told us he was her son, or nephew, or something."

"Possibly." Tony turned back to the list. "These people are bound to be ex-directory, you know, and several even live abroad. Look –" he moved his finger down the column – "Brittany, the States, Hong Kong. How on earth did he get their addresses? Pity you didn't open those letters, love."

"I couldn't have, it wouldn't have been right."

"No, I suppose not. You've not received any replies, have you?"

"Not yet, but for all we know none might have been expected."

"It'll have to remain a mystery, then," Tony said, and as the two children appeared in search of breakfast, he snapped the book shut and slipped the list into his pocket.

It was just after ten o'clock when Hannah and Webb set out for Chipping Claydon. She was feeling more relaxed than the previous evening, partly because she had David as backup, but also because, after an excellent meal, they had made love and she'd spent the night at his flat.

It was one of those April mornings when the strengthening sun brought out the blossom, birds sang, and summer seemed just round the corner. Perfect, in fact, for a drive in the country. The only disappointment was that they couldn't make a day of it, with a walk across the fields and a pub lunch. With other people to interview, David would have to return to work after seeing Nicholas.

They'd decided that when they reached the cottage, she should go in first and hear whatever it was Nicholas had to say. (It had crossed her mind that he might be thinking of leaving Pamela, and she wasn't looking forward to the meeting.) Then, when it was over, she would wait in the car while David interviewed him.

It was a while since Hannah had been out this way, and she'd forgotten how pretty it was. Fields spread on either side of them, dotted with the white blobs of the first lambs, copses were spiked with the sharp green of new growth, and several roadside cottages were in the process of being rethatched.

"How have you managed to track these people down after so long?" Hannah asked suddenly. "They must have different addresses from last time, when most of them would still have been based with their families."

"True, but we were in luck. The university lent us their Alumni booklet, which lists all graduates year by year, together with news of what they're doing now and where they're living. It saved us the hell of a lot of work. Incidentally, your pal Adam Greenwood was also there at the time, so I'll have to see him, too."

They had crossed the M4 and were driving almost due north, but at the signpost for Chipping Claydon they turned into a winding lane with width for only one vehicle. "Keep your eyes peeled for passing places," Webb remarked, "we might meet a tractor round the next corner. Once we get to the village, you'll have to direct me."

"Actually the cottage is on this road, before the village proper. Slow down a bit, I mightn't recognise it till we're past it. It can't be much farther now."

They came on it suddenly, round a bend, and Webb braked sharply. Fortunately there was nothing behind them. The wrought-iron gates were open, showing a loosely gravelled driveway at the top of which stood a green Bentley. Webb turned in and parked behind it, switching off the engine. Silence descended on them, broken only by the distant bleating of a sheep and an aeroplane droning overhead.

Hannah surveyed the cottage. The Kings had recently renovated it, in her opinion destroying most of its original character. Now it was simply a smaller, rural version of their Wimbledon home. "Wish me luck!" she said to Webb, opening the car door.

It seemed Nicholas had not heard their arrival. She walked up to the front door, her feet crunching in the gravel, and rang the bell. On the tiny lawn a blackbird was foraging for worms, unconcerned by her presence. Out on the road a car went by. She glanced back at David, but he had taken out some papers and wasn't looking in her direction.

She rang again, and bent to peer through the window by the door, originally mullioned and now double-glazed. The two downstairs rooms had been knocked into one, abnormally long and narrow. Hannah could see the patio doors at the far end, and, through them, the back garden with its paved terrace. The room itself, furnished with a chintz three-piece suite and gate-legged table, was empty.

Hannah swore under her breath. After insisting she come out to see him, the least he could do was watch out for her arrival. She moved to the corner of the house and looked down the narrow strip of grass leading round the back. Perhaps he was in the kitchen with the radio on.

David was still engrossed in his reading, so she walked briskly down the side of the house and turned the corner, passing the patio doors and their more open view of the sitting room on her way to the back door. Temper fraying by this time, she knocked briskly on it, at the same time turning the handle, which gave as the door swung inwards.

"Hello?" she called. "Nicholas, it's Hannah. Are you there?"

There was no reply. Then, as she moved inside, she saw him, sprawled over the kitchen table, his head in his arms.

"Nicholas!" she said again, more sharply. "Are you all right?" She went quickly towards him and shook him by the shoulder.

No response. Then her eyes fell on the empty whisky bottle, the glass and the scattered pills.

Fearfully she bent to peer at his face, half-hidden in the cradle of his arms. Eyes closed, he seemed to be asleep, but there was no sign of breathing that she could see. Hannah took the flaccid wrist between her fingers, but her own heart was hammering so loudly she wouldn't have felt a pulse even if there'd been one. Abandoning the attempt, she turned and ran out of the room, back down the path to the front of the house.

David looked up at her precipitate approach, and was out of the car before she reached him. "For God's sake, Hannah, what is it?"

"He's collapsed," she gasped. "In the kitchen. David – I'm not even sure he's still alive."

David raced past her and she followed, legs now weak with shock. By the time she reached the kitchen, he was bending over Nicholas, feeling the side of his neck. She leaned against the door frame, watching him, and after a minute he turned to her, shaking his head.

"I'm very sorry, Hannah, there's nothing we can do."

"But – there must be! I mean, he wouldn't have – he wanted to speak to me." Oh why, she agonised, hadn't she come last night, as he'd asked her?

Dimly she was aware of David taking out his mobile and giving instructions. She levered herself away from the door frame and moved cautiously forward. Only then did she catch sight of the paper, a small white triangle just visible under one of the outspread arms. Putting a finger on it, she slid it out to lie exposed on the table, and was startled to see her own name. *Sorry, Hannah*, she read, *I couldn't wait after all. Nicholas.*

She put a hand to her mouth, and David, slipping his mobile into his pocket, rejoined her. As he put his arm round her, she wordlessly indicated the note, and equally silently he read it.

"There's an envelope addressed to his wife, too," he said then. "He's lying on it, but I saw it when I was feeling for a pulse.

Come on, love, you wait in the car. I'm going to be tied up here for some time, but I'll arrange for someone to take you home."

Hannah reached out to pick up the note, but Webb shook his head. "We can't touch anything," he said, and she let herself be led out of the open door and back to the car. The blackbird was still digging in the grass.

Webb got in with her. "I'll stay till the boys arrive. There's nothing I can do in there."

Hannah said through juddering lips, "This might have been prevented if I'd come last night."

"You can't blame yourself. It looks as though he was intending to do it all along, hence the pills and booze. He wanted to justify himself to someone, that's all. Perhaps he's now done so in the note to his wife, which is as it should be anyway."

Hannah said miserably, "If I'd liked him, I might have made the effort – asked you to hold up dinner or something. But, as always, he got my back up, expecting me to drop everything at a moment's notice." She shivered. "I hate to think of him dying here all alone."

"It was his choice, Hannah. He could just as easily have done this at home."

"It would be to spare Pamela – he couldn't let her find him. That's what he meant by phoning me because I'm her friend."

"He said that?"

She nodded. "Though why he didn't ring Paula, I can't think."

"Perhaps she's away?"

Hannah looked at him, stricken. "I never thought of that."

It seemed a long time before the first of the police cars arrived and the driveway behind her began to fill with men. David went to meet them and after a terse account of the circumstances, she heard him add, "Miss James lives in my block of flats. She had a phone call from Mr King asking her to meet him, and was disturbed by his manner. She reported it to me, and as I had to interview him in connection with the Lester case, I came out with her. Thank God I did."

156

Which explanation of her presence, Hannah thought, might or might not be accepted. Just as well Sergeant – or rather, Inspector – Jackson wasn't with them. She'd seen a twinkle in his eye more than once, and was sure he suspected the truth about their relationship.

More and more cars were now arriving, drawing up on to the verge of the narrow road so as not to cause more obstruction than necessary. Eventually David came and opened the passenger door. He gave her a private wink and said formally, "DC Wright will run you home, Miss James. I'm sorry you've had such an unpleasant experience."

He helped her out of the car.

"Who's going to let Pamela know?" she asked him.

"The local police will call round. Unfortunately, this is something they're used to."

"Should I try Paula? If she's home, she'd want to go over as soon as possible."

"That would be a good idea."

As they talked, they'd been walking back to the road, where one of the cars was waiting for her with its door open. DC Wright, she was relieved to see, was, despite his rank, a man of about fifty with a comfortable paunch, a kindly face and a disappearing hairline. David had probably guessed that under the circumstances she'd feel more comfortable with him than with a fresh-faced young officer. She gave him a grateful smile as she got into the car.

The constable waited while she strapped herself in and then set off, driving on into the village in order to turn the car. They circumnavigated the duck pond, watched by interested groups of spectators who had noticed all the activity up the road, and then, thankfully, they were headed for Shillingham. As they passed the Kings' cottage, Hannah had a swift glimpse of David walking back up the path talking earnestly to one of his men.

She had let Nicholas down, she thought bleakly. He had appealed to her for – what? Help? Sympathy? Understanding?

157

Whatever it was, she'd denied him. And she'd have to live with that.

DC Wright's homely Broadshire voice interrupted her musings. "Have a mint, miss," he offered, passing her a tube. "They always have a steadying influence, I find."

Hannah extracted one with a shaky smile and settled down for the journey back to Shillingham.

"There's always the possibility that it wasn't suicide," Webb was saying, "though on the face of it, it looks straightforward enough – pills, whisky, notes, the classic combination. The notes could be fakes, of course: the handwriting will settle it, but in my opinion they're genuine. And while a crafty killer might leave a note for the wife, he couldn't, surely, have known about Miss James."

"Unless he overheard the phone call. You say the back door was unlocked, Guv?"

"Yes; King was expecting her this morning. Obviously he meant her to find him, but at least he was decent enough to die tidily."

"*Sorry, Hannah, I couldn't wait after all*," Dawson read. "Do we know Miss James's relationship with the deceased?"

"Acquaintances only, he was married to a friend of hers. The interesting thing, though, is that he was at Broadshire Uni when the Lester boy went missing. Odd, wouldn't you say, that he should top himself just when the remains have been discovered?"

Dawson pursed his lips. "Perhaps he knew something about it."

"If he did, it's more than we do," Webb commented glumly.

The standard procedure swung into operation: the Coroner's Officer arrived, followed by the police surgeon and Scenes of Crime officers. Finally, while the body was being photographed, the pathologist, Dr Stapleton, appeared. He was a small, irritable man with a dried-up air about him. As the photographer respectfully moved aside he walked slowly round the kitchen table, pulling thoughtfully at his lower lip as he observed the body from all angles. He then made a cursory examination of it before turning to Webb.

"Not going to ask how long he's been dead, I hope, Superintendent?"

"I know you too well, Doctor. Mind, a rough guess would be helpful, to give us a start."

The pathologist grunted. "Hardly a scientific approach. Still, I can tell you that rigor mortis is present in the face and jaw but it hasn't progressed far." He glanced round the room. "So as there are no radiators in here and it's reasonably cool, I'd say between seven and eight hours. However, a detailed examination might give us a totally different angle."

"But if you're right, that would be the early hours of the morning. A popular time for suicides."

"If it is a suicide," Stapleton reminded him, pursing his small mouth. "Well, if there's nothing else I'll be on my way. I'll see you at the mortuary in due course."

The Shillingham one this time, Webb reflected, and a more gory post-mortem in prospect than that of young Lester and his bones. King had died fully clothed, which meant he'd made no attempt to go to bed the previous night. What had he been doing during those long hours between his phone call to Hannah and his death? Had someone been here with him? Had he made any more phone calls? Some of these questions would resolve themselves, others might remain unanswered. In any event, Webb hoped Hannah wasn't continuing to blame herself. She couldn't have foreseen this.

He remained at the scene until, the photographer and SOCOs having finished with the body, it was sealed in a bag and removed to the waiting hearse.

Had King's death anything to do with Lester's? he wondered yet again, wishing futilely that he'd been able to catch the man at home the previous day. His wife hadn't mentioned that he was coming down here. Perhaps she hadn't known? Or had it, God forbid, been the passing on of Webb's message that had precipitated events? Whatever, King had managed to elude him and the widow would now have to be seen instead. Though that would fall to someone else, thank God.

In the meantime, Webb's own schedule had been totally disrupted. He'd hoped at least to have spoken to Adam Greenwood today, since he was virtually on the doorstep. That would now have to wait till tomorrow.

He looked at his watch. Three o'clock. He'd have liked to look round the cottage while he was here, but it was still being taped and powdered for traces of an alien presence. Tomorrow, perhaps.

"I'm going now," he told the men in white coats. "Let me know if anything unexpected turns up." And he walked out to the car in which he and Hannah had unsuspectingly driven there nearly five hours ago.

Paula Welling said increduously, "But I just can't believe it! What would make him do a thing like that?"

"I don't know," Hannah answered soberly. "Perhaps he'd received some bad news – a medical prognosis, something like that." She paused. "I did wonder," she added tentatively, "why he contacted me rather than you."

"Well, that's soon answered," Paula said flatly. "Nicholas and I didn't get on. We never have. Mutual jealousy, perhaps. Pamela tried at first to bring us together, but eventually she gave up and we just meet when he's not around. You could be right about a prognosis; he'd go to pieces if he heard anything like that. About Pamela, though; do you think the police will have seen her by now?"

"I should imagine so. Paula, I'm so sorry."

"I'll give her a ring to say I'm on my way. Thanks, Hannah. I'm sorry you drew the short straw in this."

"What about the cats?" Hannah asked.

"A neighbour will feed them. Anyway, I'm hoping to come more or less straight back and bring Pammy with me."

"Give her my love, and if there's anything—"
"Yes, I know. Thanks."

Naomi stared at the young policewoman on the step. "*What* did you say?"

"That you were right, Miss Ryder. I was asked to let you know."

"It was *Nigel* who broke into the Greenwoods' flat?"

"Nigel Packard, yes. And the objects you reported missing were found in his flat. I'm afraid you can't have them back yet, but once everything's been cleared up, they'll be returned to you."

"Thank you," Naomi said numbly.

"Thank *you*. Without your help we'd probably never have caught him – he hasn't been in trouble before."

Naomi nodded, and after a moment the young woman smiled and turned away. Naomi watched her walk down the path and turn left towards the High Street. Only when the sound of her footsteps had died away did she close the door and go slowly back upstairs.

What had she done? Oh God, what had she done? She'd not really believed Nigel was involved; in fact, she'd been hoping for confirmation that he wasn't. *He's never been in trouble before.* Now, thanks to her and her petty spite, he would have a police record. If they sent him to prison, he'd probably never write another line, and it would be her fault – she who prided herself on encouraging the arts.

She reached her flat and stood looking about her as though disorientated. If only she knew his address, she could write to explain. But she didn't, and she could hardly ask the police for it. What must he be thinking of her? It was easy to guess. If only they hadn't watched Adam's bloody programme, none of this would have happened. It was talk of the spoons that had done it – that and Nigel's dreams of avarice.

There was another side to it, too; the family had always

161

warned her against taking in people about whom she knew nothing. Now, they had been vindicated. Though they mightn't actually say, 'We told you so', it would be in their faces.

Naomi sat down at the kitchen table and wept.

It was almost nine o'clock by the time Webb arrived home. After making out his own report, he'd stayed on to read Chris Ledbetter's on his interviews of the previous day.

The conflicting opinions on Piers Lester had intrigued him. Granted, there was often disparity in descriptions of a victim, but not usually as divergent as this. The landlady, of course, had taken him at face value, unquestioningly repeating his claims of popularity, importunate girlfriends and party invitations. On the other hand, the personal tutor spoke of almost universal dislike, but a seeming unawareness of it. How accurate a perception was that? Had the young man suffered secretly at his ostracism, or genuinely been too thick-skinned to notice it? Webb hoped the latter.

A group photograph had been clipped to one of the pages, with the words *Trinity Term 1972* scrawled on the back. In pencil, Chris had added *End one on the right, second row*.

Webb had reached for a magnifying glass and studied Piers Lester long and hard. The slightness of build Stapleton had deduced was confirmed in the flesh, but though shorter than his colleagues, Lester's smile was strikingly self-confident – cocky, almost – an impression underlined by the tilt of the head, and his fair hair, in the longish style of the times, flopped over his forehead with what looked like artful nonchalance. Perhaps it was only hindsight that hinted at a larger gap between him and the man on his right than separated the other students. Body language? Possibly.

Webb had then moved his glass along the rows of youthful faces, curious to see if Nicholas King was among them. He found him almost at once, tall and stooping even then, his fine hair unbecomingly straggly. And next to him stood a young Adam

162

Greenwood, eyes narrowed against the sun, his dark, intelligent face much the same as today.

How many more of his interviewees would be in this group? Webb wondered, but though pictures of some had appeared in the press, he was not familiar enough with them to recognise them from more than twenty years ago.

Was it coincidence that both the men whose mortal remains he'd seen this week were on this photograph? There seemed little else to link the gifted but irritating man Hannah had described with the unpopular student who, had he lived, would have gone down without a degree.

The seemingly insoluble puzzles facing them were what had happened to Piers Lester on that summer night twenty-seven years ago, and how, either alive or dead, he'd arrived in Fox Woods, some ten miles from where he was last seen.

A tap on the door roused Webb from his musings, and he opened it to find Hannah outside. She still looked pale, and his conscience stirred.

"How are you, love? I was going to phone, but I've only just got in."

"I'm all right." She preceded him into the living room and walked to the window, staring, from this elevated vantage point, over the rooftops to the lights of the town at the foot of the hill.

"Were you able to get hold of Paula?" Webb asked, handing her a drink.

"Yes." She turned from the window. "The reason Nicholas didn't phone her was that they didn't get on. Anyway, she's going straight up to Pamela's." She hesitated. "Pamela will get that note he left, won't she?"

"Yes, but not immediately. In cases like this, I'm afraid personal considerations go out of the window."

She looked at him steadily. "You've read it?"

"Yes."

"And it didn't – give any explanation?"

"No, except, a psychiatrist might say, of his state of mind."

"Yet another mystery, then."

"We'll check with his doctor to see if he'd any serious illness, and his finances will have to be examined, too."

"I doubt that there's any problem there."

"Unless he'd been gambling on the stock market and lost a packet. You never know what will turn up in cases like this."

"Well, whatever it was he's out of it now," Hannah said, with a spurt of irritation. "If anything has to be faced – quite apart from all the publicity – it's poor Pamela who'll have to deal with it."

She looked down into her glass. "Do you think he really wanted to talk to me, or was just ensuring that he'd be found?"

Webb shrugged. "It's anybody's guess."

"If he'd told me what was troubling him, I might have been able to help. In which case, he'd be alive now."

"Darling, ifs and might-have-beens are doubtful commodities. For what it's worth, though, I really don't think you'd have changed his mind; he'd come prepared, with the pills and whisky. He meant to kill himself, whether he spoke to you first or not."

"The trouble is, I can't get that note out of my head: *Sorry, I couldn't wait.* As though my putting off going was the last straw." Her voice broke and Webb put his arms round her. For several minutes they stood close together in the silent room, simply holding each other. Then Hannah moved back, looking up into his face with a smile.

"Thanks. I needed that."

"Any time," he said.

"Do you think you'll ever find out why he did it?"

"If we don't, it won't be for want of trying."

After she'd gone he poured himself another drink and settled into his favourite chair. Nor would it be for want of trying if they didn't solve the Lester case. However, the trail was cold there, and all their enquiries so far had led to dead ends – literally, in King's case, he thought grimly. Perhaps Adam Greenwood would shed some light on it tomorrow. He could only hope so.

Twelve

S unday morning, and Eva and Verity were strolling round the strip of garden which had been screened off for their private use.

"Mainly flowering shrubs, I think," Eva said, "with just a few annuals for a splash of colour here and there. We mustn't go mad, though, or we'll be spending all our time on our knees!"

"Russell said we could borrow their gardener," Verity reminded her, but as she'd expected, Eva dismissed the suggestion.

"The whole point of having our own plot is that we can potter about in it. Let's go to the garden centre on our way back from lunch; their bedding plants are sure to be in by now."

To both women's relief, there'd been no invitation this week to Sunday lunch next door; the last thing they wanted was for Russell and Louise to feel obliged to invite them, which in any case would have been contrary to the 'rules' drawn up when they'd agreed to share the house. Today, they planned to drive out to a country pub.

"I fancy a bower of some kind at the far end," Eva continued, "where we can sit looking back towards the house. We could train something sweet-smelling over it."

She glanced at her friend. "You're very quiet today. Still thinking of that business with Naomi's lodger?"

Verity sighed. "Yes, I was. As you know, I've always been uneasy about these people she invites into her home. They never pay their way, and I'm sure this one's not the first to help himself to her things. But at least, to our knowledge, none of the others have been housebreakers and worse. Suppose something really serious had happened to Mia – or Naomi, come to that."

Eva took her arm. "Well, it didn't, thank God, so try to put it out of your mind. Let's hope it's at least made Naomi think twice, and she won't be so ready to adopt lame ducks in future. Now, what do you think about some philadelphus along the trellis?"

"Mrs Greenwood? Detective Superintendent Webb. Sorry to disturb you on a Sunday, but I phoned earlier."

"Yes, of course. My husband's expecting you." Imogen showed him into the handsome but still sparsely furnished room. At the far end, patio doors stood open and Webb could see Adam Greenwood sitting on the terrace with the Sunday papers; which would not, he reflected, be reporting the news of King's death; this would break in roughly an hour's time, at a press conference to be held at Carrington Street.

"Adam –" Imogen walked down the room and her husband turned at the sound of her voice – "the Superintendent's here."

Greenwood rose quickly and came inside, his hand held out. Webb, taking it, weighed the television image against the living man, noting the quick, decisive movements, the alert gaze and easy smile which had so charmed Hannah. His social persona, no doubt.

"Could I bring you some coffee, Superintendent?" Imogen asked, still hovering.

"That would be welcome, thank you."

"Please sit down." Greenwood indicated an easy chair, and as Webb did so, seated himself opposite. "I suppose you want to talk about Piers Lester? I'm afraid there's not much I can tell you; I hardly knew him."

"It's specifically the day he disappeared that interests us," Webb began. "You must have been asked this before, but can you remember the last time you saw him?"

"To be honest, I'm not sure I can. Piers wasn't someone you noticed."

166

"Perhaps you could try, sir?" Webb suggested.

Adam Greenwood held his gaze for a moment, then said lightly, "Let me think, now. He was probably in the refectory at lunchtime. In fact now I think of it, I believe I caught a glimpse of him leaving."

"Could it have been tea rather than lunch?" Lester had been seen there at teatime.

"No, I never went to the refectory for tea."

Not a last sighting, then. All the same: "Did you happen to notice which direction he went in?"

Greenwood moved impatiently. "I thought I'd made myself clear, Superintendent: I wasn't interested in the man, and I certainly didn't spend my time watching his every movement."

He broke off as his wife came in with some coffee, and Webb saw the alarmed look she flashed him as she set down the tray.

Imogen, uneasy at the atmosphere between the men, would have liked to stay and listen, but neither invited her to do so, and with a murmured excuse she left the room. One of the flat's disadvantages was that there was nowhere for her to go apart from the bedroom or the kitchen, and she was suddenly claustrophobic.

Impulsively she went out of the front door and walked round the side of the house, past Elliott's doorway, to the back garden. The spring sunshine was warm on her back and as she strolled down the lawn past the newly planted flowers, she was aware of voices from behind the trellis at the far side. Eva and Verity.

Imogen wished passionately that she was closer to her mother-in-law, that she could go to her and pour out all her nebulous worries about Adam. For although their brief coolness was over, he was obviously still deeply troubled.

Which was no doubt why he'd snapped at the Superintendent just now. While passing Webb his coffee, Imogen had taken rapid stock of the man who'd provoked that outburst, and her assessment had not been reassuring; the tall, loose-limbed detective whom she'd admitted had seemed pleasant enough, with his unexpectedly attractive smile. But on closer inspection the grey eyes were disconcertingly shrewd and the mouth, when not smiling, was hard. She was sure he'd be excellent at his job, and for some reason this frightened her.

Inside the flat, Adam said more placatingly, "I'm sorry, but I did warn you I wouldn't be much help."

"How did you yourself spend that afternoon?" Webb asked casually, aware, though he wasn't looking at him, that Greenwood had stiffened.

"I?"

Webb nodded.

There was a pause, then Greenwood said, "I went back to the house with some friends. We were having a party that night and there were preparations to make."

"Did you return to the campus that day?"

"No, I did not. Why the sudden interest in me, Superintendent?"

"Because it's you I'm interviewing, sir," Webb replied blandly. "Everyone else concerned will be asked the same questions."

"I see. Yes, of course. Well, we went into town and bought some food and booze and then returned to the house and cleared the downstairs for dancing."

"Who did you share the house with?"

Greenwood's eyebrow lifted but he made no further demur. "Andrew North, Gregory Blaise and Jeremy Painswick."

"And how many guests were there?"

"About two dozen, I suppose. We limited it to close friends, since it was the last time we'd all be together."

"Was Felix Lytton one of them?"

Greenwood looked surprised. "Yes, as it happens."

"And there were girls, of course?"

"Of course."

"But not Carla Keating?"

Greenwood's eyes narrowed. "What do you know about her?"

"That she'd been Lytton's girlfriend until he had a fight with Lester over her."

"Oh, now look," Greenwood protested quickly, "that wasn't as it sounds."

"Then how was it, sir?"

"Well . . ." For the first time, Greenwood was floundering. "Felix did go around with Carla, yes."

"And she did go out with Lester?"

"Only once, for a stupid dare."

"All I'm saying is there could have been no love lost between the two men."

"It blew over very quickly."

"But Lytton broke up with Carla because of it?"

"You have been busy, Superintendent," Greenwood said acidly. "However, if you're hoping to uncover smouldering hatred you're barking up the wrong tree. Felix was very laid back about the whole thing. The relationship wouldn't have lasted beyond the end of term, anyway."

It corresponded with what he'd read of the tutor's statement. As usual, no new leads. Webb decided to play his trump card.

"Was Nicholas King also there that evening?"

Greenwood looked amused. "You're really interested in the party, aren't you? I can't think why, but to answer your question, yes, he was."

"One of your close friends, then?"

"At university, yes. We lost touch later."

"All the same, I imagine you'll be sorry to hear he's dead."

Adam Greenwood stared at him speechlessly.

"He was found yesterday morning," Webb continued. "He appears to have taken his own life, though at this stage we can't rule out the possibility of foul play."

Greenwood moistened white lips. "But – he can't be. I saw him on Friday."

Webb looked up quickly. "You saw him, sir? I thought you said you'd lost touch?"

Greenwood swallowed, regretting the unguarded admission. "We had, but I spent the day in London and – happened to run into him. We'd not seen each other since we came down."

"Quite a coincidence that, isn't it?"

"A damnable one," Greenwood said in a low voice. He got up abruptly and went over to a table where some bottles were arrayed. "Drink, Superintendent?"

"No, thank you."

"Forgive me, but I need one." He drained it in one draught.

"What were you doing in London, sir?" Webb braced himself for another protest, but Greenwood was in shock and answered automatically.

"I went to Broadcasting House, to check something for this week's programme."

"And then?"

His eyes flickered. "I met – a friend for lunch."

"Who would that have been, sir?"

There was a long silence. Then he said expressionlessly, "Jeremy Painswick."

"The MP, who'd shared the house with you? Quite a day for reunions, wasn't it? Where did you lunch?"

"The Café Royal."

"And did Mr King join you?"

"No, he'd another engagement."

"How did he seem when you met?"

"All right. My God, I can't take this in."

"Did he give the impression of being upset about anything?"

Greenwood made a dismissive gesture. "Nicholas has always been highly strung. The least thing upset him." His fist was convulsively clenching and unclenching at his side. This had hit him harder than Webb had expected, and he wondered why. "Who found him, his wife?"

"As a matter of fact, I did."

Greenwood said blankly, "You? But—"

"He has a cottage not far from here."

170

"And that's where he was?" There was incredulity in his eyes.

"Yes; he must have driven down straight after seeing you. Have you any idea why he should do that?"

"None at all," Greenwood said explosively. "It just doesn't make sense."

"Unless he came expressly to kill himself. If, of course, that's what happened."

The man flinched and turned away, staring through the still-open windows to where his wife could be seen at the far end of the garden. Then, as a thought struck him, he turned back.

"Did he leave a note?"

"For his wife, yes."

"You don't—?" Greenwood broke off, thinking better of the question. "This is terrible," he said instead. Then, "How did he do it?"

No point in being secretive; the papers would have it in an hour. "Alcohol and barbiturates." Webb got to his feet. "Well, if there's nothing else you can tell me, I won't take up any more of your time. Sorry to have been the bearer of bad news."

Greenwood scarcely seemed to have heard him. In silence he escorted Webb to the front door and showed him out. Webb had taken barely a couple of steps on to the gravel when the door closed behind him.

It would be interesting, he thought, easing his way through the stile gate, to find out exactly when Greenwood was at the BBC, what time he reached the Café Royal and which train he caught back to Broadshire. Because Webb was prepared to bet there was a large chunk of his day that Adam Greenwood had not told him about, and he intended to find out what it was.

Hannah was also paying a visit that morning. Gwen needed to be told what had happened, and it was something Hannah didn't want to explain either over the phone or during the hectic schedule of the school day.

Accordingly, just after eleven, she drove down the hill to Park

171

Road and the little house where, in the past, she and Gwen had so often hammered out timetables and discussed staff problems.

Soon it would be up for sale. Gwen's mother, who was to have moved to her other daughter's when Gwen left for Canada, had taken matters into her own hands by dying during the winter. She'd been in frail health and almost blind, and Hannah was glad for her sake that she'd been able to die in her own home.

It was Bruce Cameron who opened the door, his shock of grey hair as unruly as ever, his blue eyes twinkling as he saw her.

"Hannah! What a pleasant surprise! Come on in and have a sherry."

The front room which, for as long as Hannah could remember, had been old Mrs Rutherford's domain, had, since her death, been redecorated and a lot of the over-large furniture removed. The result was altogether more airy and welcoming. Gwen looked up from a newspaper.

"Hello, Hannah. What brings you here?"

She at least was unchanged, Hannah thought gratefully. No one would have guessed that this gawky woman, with diffident brown eyes and hair which continually escaped its French pleat, was in fact a brilliant intellectual with a will of iron. It was largely to Gwen Cameron that Ashbourne owed its excellent reputation.

"I'm sorry to intrude on a Sunday," Hannah said, accepting the sherry Bruce handed her, "but I've some rather sad news, I'm afraid."

She sat down, aware of their instant attention. "It's Nicholas King. I'm sorry to tell you that he – died yesterday."

"Oh, poor Pamela!" Gwen exclaimed. "Was it his heart?"

"Actually he – he took his own life." Hannah stared down into her sherry glass. "And I found him."

Over their exclamations of concern, she related the story of driving out there 'with a police officer who happens to live at Beechcroft' and finding Nicholas's body.

"Thank God the policeman was with you," Gwen said, "though I don't quite see *why* he was."

172

"Well, as I said, Nicholas had phoned on Friday evening wanting me to go straight out there. Though obviously I never thought he'd kill himself, he sounded – strange, and you know, Gwen, how difficult and temperamental he can be at times. *Could* be," she corrected herself after a minute.

"I happened to see Superintendent Webb and mentioned I was apprehensive about driving out there, and as luck would have it, it turned out he wanted to see Nicholas himself."

Cameron frowned. "Why the hell?"

"Because he was at university with this Lester boy whose bones have been found."

"You're not saying there's any connection?" Gwen asked in bewilderment.

"The police have reopened the case – you must have read about it. They're re-interviewing everyone they spoke to when Lester disappeared, now that he's known to have died at about that time."

"I meant, any connection with Nicholas's death. But that's ridiculous – there can't be. How ghastly for you, though, to come upon him like that."

"Yes. And I can't help wondering whether, if I'd gone there on Friday, I might have been able to dissuade him."

Bruce Cameron laid a kindly hand on her shoulder. "You mustn't feel that way, honey; you weren't to know how his mind was working. Gwen, my love, I don't think Hannah should be alone today. I'm sure lunch would stretch to three?"

"Of course it would. You must stay, Hannah."

"That's sweet of you, but I can't – I mean, I never intended—"

"That's settled then," Bruce said firmly, and Hannah, more than grateful to have company, smilingly capitulated.

The post-mortem on Monday morning revealed that death was due to a combination of alcohol and barbiturates and there was no suggestion of foul play. It was concluded, therefore, that Nicholas King's death was self-inflicted, but Webb was no longer concerned with his health or the state of his bank balance. He was as sure as he could be that the man's death was a direct result of his having met Adam Greenwood in London last Friday.

On his return from the mortuary he spent some time on the telephone, liaising with the Met and arranging for his men to go up to London to check Greenwood's story. Of the names Webb himself had been asked to contact, there'd originally been four in the London area, but that of Gregory Blaise had been scored through, with the word 'deceased' alongside it. Now Nicholas King's could also be deleted, which left the two Webb most wanted to see, Jeremy Painswick and Felix Lytton.

Using the invaluable Alumni magazine, Webb phoned both men. The House being in recess, Painswick was at home, and although he prevaricated, he finally agreed to see Webb at his house in Richmond at four thirty.

Felix Lytton took more tracking down, and Webb was given a succession of telephone numbers before finally locating him at a meeting in the City. He also seemed less than anxious to be interviewed, but since he lived in Kingston, only a few miles from Painswick, he eventually agreed to be home by five thirty, and to see Webb then.

Webb put down the phone and glanced at his watch. It was now midday; he must allow at least an hour and a half to drive to London and locate the Richmond house – possibly an hour and three-quarters. Which left plenty of time for a read-through of the remaining reports and a leisurely lunch at the Brown Bear.

There was a tap on the door and Inspector Jackson put his head round it. "Not disturbing you, am I, Guv?"

"Ken! Good to see you! Come in."

"Fact is, I've just finished with the Lonsdale case and I was wondering if you could do with an extra hand."

"I certainly could. Things are moving quite fast at the moment; I'm off to London shortly to see a couple of men who seem relevant to both cases. I was going to take Marshbanks, but if you're free, so much the better. You can drive, and I'll outline various theories and bounce them off you."

Jackson grinned. "Fine by me. It'll be just like old times."

"Give me half an hour to sort this lot out, then over lunch I'll fill you in with the latest developments."

"Ma? It's Elliott. How are things?"

"Hello, darling. Fine, fine. Wasn't it a glorious weekend? I had Sonia and the children to lunch, and we were able to eat in the garden. It's looking really colourful now."

Elliott wasn't interested in either children or gardens. "This is to let you know I'll be down on Wednesday for the rest of the week. I really must get the flat organised, so I'm bringing a camp bed with me and will spend my time scouring the auction rooms and second-hand furniture emporiums. I know you enjoyed going to auctions with Pa, and I thought you might like to tag along."

"Sounds fun – of course I should. I suppose Maggie can't get away?"

"No, which is why I want to be back for the weekend. By the way, did you hear any more of Adam's would-be burglar?"

"Oh – yes." Eva was thankful Verity wasn't in the room. "It turned out to be a man who'd been lodging with Naomi."

"Good God!"

"He sounded a dubious character – had pinched things from her in the past – but you know Naomi. If she thinks they have an ounce of talent in their little finger, she'll turn a blind eye and bend over backwards to help them."

"Did they nab him at her place, then?"

"No, he'd done a bunk the day of the attack and she hasn't seen him since. That's what made her suspicious. In fact, it was she who pointed the police in his direction, which I admit surprised me."

"And was it those wretched spoons that were the attraction?"

"It seems so, yes."

"Mia still OK – no repercussions later?"

"No, she's fine, as far as I know. She went back to school last week."

"Right; well, I'll aim to be down about lunchtime on Wednesday. Suppose we have a pub meal and then get stuck in on the furniture hunt?"

"Lovely. I'll be ready. See you then, darling."

The drive up the M4 was boring but uneventful and took them to within a few miles of their destination.

"Posh place, isn't it?" Jackson commented, as they drove down the wide tree-lined roads past detached houses in sizeable gardens. "Chestnut Avenue, you said? Should be next on the left."

It was. Southcot was one of the more substantial houses, with a small pond and fountain in the front garden. Its gates were firmly closed, and Jackson perforce parked at the kerb.

"Welcome!" he murmured under his breath.

They walked together up the long drive, conscious that their approach might well be under observation from the downstairs windows. "Remember, Ken," Webb said wryly, "in the Chief Super's book Painswick's a VIP and must be treated with kid gloves."

"I'll try to restrain myself, Guv!"

They were admitted by a plain-looking woman in a blue dress, who escorted them to one of the closed doors and knocked on it.

"Superintendent Webb and Inspector Jackson, sir," she announced.

If Jeremy Painswick was uneasy about the meeting, he gave no sign of it. Tall and sandy-haired, he had the pale eyebrows and lashes that went with such colouring, and an exceptionally white skin. He was wearing a pale green shirt with a cravat tucked into the neck, and dark green cord trousers.

"Superintendent – Inspector – do come in. Sorry you've had such a long journey; make yourselves comfortable, and Margaret will bring in some tea."

Pity they didn't have a baby with them, Jackson thought sardonically, so that he could have kissed it.

"Now, gentlemen, how can I help you?" Painswick leaned towards them with a pleasantly encouraging expression, just as though, Webb thought, he were conducting a surgery at his constituency.

Time to take the reins into his own hands, he decided, but paused as the woman returned with a silver tray containing sandwiches and scones as well as the promised tea. He saw Jackson's eyes light up, and hid a smile.

Once cups, saucers and plates had been distributed and sandwiches taken – for all the world like a vicarage tea party – Painswick sat back in his chair. "So, Superintendent, I gather you want to discuss Piers Lester?"

"And also Nicholas King, sir." That shook him, Webb noted with satisfaction.

"Yes, indeed, I heard about his death on the news. Quite a shock."

"You'd seen him recently?" Webb asked. Though his tone was casual, his eyes were intent on the man's face and he caught the almost imperceptible ripple which warned him that Painswick was about to lie.

"No, unfortunately we all lost touch when we left university. I've several of his CDs, though. Brilliant pianist."

"I believe Mr Adam Greenwood met him last Friday?"

"So he told me. Quite a coincidence."

"Seeing him just before he died? Yes, it was."

Painswick flicked a wary glance at him but made no comment.

"And what about Mr Greenwood? You'd presumably kept in touch with him?"

"Well, no, actually."

"Don't tell me *you* just happened to run into each other, too?" Webb's voice was heavy with irony, and Painswick flushed.

"No, I'd phoned to congratulate him on his BAFTA award, and the call was transferred to his flat in Shillingham. When he

177

mentioned he was coming up on Friday, we arranged to have lunch."

It sounded a little too pat to Webb.

"Did anyone else join you?"

That uneasy ripple again. "No, it was just the two of us."

"What about Felix Lytton?"

Painswick's hand stilled over his plate. "What about him, Superintendent?"

"You must have seen him over the years? He lives just down the road, in a manner of speaking."

"As a matter of fact, I haven't." But he wasn't meeting Webb's eyes. "We've really nothing in common any more," he added.

There was little else to get out of him on that, Webb decided. He moved on to the Lester disappearance, hearing virtually the same story that he'd had from Greenwood. He'd expected no less; doubtless they'd conferred. The interview came to a natural conclusion, and with political-type handshaking all round Webb and Jackson were shown the door.

"Sorry I'm not in his constituency," Jackson remarked, fastening his seat-belt. "I'd like the pleasure of not voting for him."

"Come, come, Ken, after all those lovely sandwiches?"

Jackson grinned shamefacedly. His insatiable appetite was legendary, though there was no indication of it in his slight frame.

They drove on to Kingston-upon-Thames, and the even more luxurious house of Felix Lytton, proprietor of a string of newspapers and television companies. This time the intricately patterned iron gates stood open – there were in fact two entrances, with a curved driveway linking them – and Jackson drove in with a flourish and parked by the front door.

Uniformed staff here, and an opulent drawing room with windows looking on to the river at the bottom of the garden. Felix Lytton was a tall, heavy man with a red face and thinning hair, and looked older than those of his contemporaries whom Webb had seen, either alive or dead.

178

"Can I offer you some tea, gentlemen?" he asked, as they sank into huge armchairs.

"Thank you no, we've just had some with Mr Painswick."

"Ah yes, you said you were calling there. Jeremy Painswick! There's a name from the past! But if I may say so, Superintendent, you're wasting your time; we told the police all we knew about Piers at the time."

"Were you surprised, sir, when Mr Lester's remains were found?"

Lytton shrugged. "Not really. After so long, it seemed obvious he must be dead."

"I believe you had a contretemps with him over a young lady?"

Lytton smiled. "Who's been talking out of turn? Jeremy? Yes, I admit I laid into him, but I heard later it was Carla who'd made the running. For a dare, would you believe? I should have been grateful to Piers – I was well shot of her."

"You actually came to blows, though?"

"I knocked him down, yes, but that was the end of it."

Yet again, Webb listened to the story of the last day of term, which was substantially the same as the other versions. And, like Painswick, Lytton confirmed that there'd been no contact with his erstwhile colleagues over the years.

"You know how it is, Superintendent. You promise to keep in touch, but you move on into different circles, new interests, and you seldom do. A pity, but life goes on."

A less revealing interview than Painwick's, Webb felt as they drove away. He looked out of the window at the mansions with their balustrades and columns, their immaculate flower-beds and manicured lawns.

"Know what, Ken?" he said suddenly. "I have an irresistible urge to slum it. Let's stop at the first chippie we come to, and sit and eat them in the car out of newspaper."

"You're behind the times, Guv, it's white paper bags now."

"Whatever. With plenty of salt and vinegar."

"You're on!" Jackson said happily, and put his foot down on the accelerator.

Eva was brushing her hair prior to going down for supper when the phone rang, and she lifted her bedroom extension.

"Hello?"

"Hello, Eva, it's Sonia."

"My dear."

"You asked me to let you know if I remembered where I'd heard of the Twelve Apostles."

Eva stiffened, her hand tightening on the receiver. "Yes?"

"It's rather an anticlimax, I'm afraid; and it's not surprising I couldn't remember – it was *years* ago, when Adam and I first started going out while he was still at university."

"Yes?" Eva repeated aridly.

"Well, it was just what he and a group of friends called themselves, that's all."

Eva closed her eyes. "They called themselves the Twelve Apostles?"

"Apparently. It was a kind of joke, really, because there were twelve of them. Adam said the second definition of 'apostle' was 'a leader or outstanding figure', which he thought most appropriate."

"I see. Well, thank you for telling me, dear."

"Right. Thanks again for Saturday. Goodbye."

Eva put the phone down and stared blindly at herself in the mirror. At least that explained the look which had passed between Adam and Russell at Sunday lunch; Russell had been been up at the same time, and would have known about the nickname. But a much more worrying question had now arisen; were those the Apostles Mr Morrison had spoken of with his dying breath? And if so, why were they so important to him?

Thirteen

The next morning, reports were on Webb's desk from the men who'd been tracing Greenwood's movements in London. It was confirmed that he had arrived at Broadcasting House at ten thirty and stayed for half an hour. The doorman had obtained a taxi for him, and fortunately the driver, a BBC regular, had been easy to trace.

Yes, he remembered picking up Mr Greenwood; he'd dropped him off at the Cicero Club in Piccadilly.

Webb tapped his pen thoughtfully. Then he reached for the well-thumbed edition of *Who's Who* and read Adam Greenwood's entry, noting that although he belonged to several London clubs the Cicero was apparently not one of them. Which meant he must have been the guest of a member – Jeremy Painswick?

Webb turned to the MP's entry; he did not list the Cicero either, and nor, as Webb discovered a minute later, did Felix Lytton. Further investigation was needed.

It was, however, confirmed that Painswick had booked a table for two for one o'clock at the Café Royal, an appointment which had been kept. So what had Greenwood been doing at the Cicero Club for over an hour last Friday? And who had been his host?

Strange how things worked out, Webb reflected. If Adam Greenwood had not let slip that he'd met King in London, his enquiries would have been running on totally different lines. The man must be cursing himself, he thought with satisfaction.

Still, today had its share of interviews, too. Webb studied the list of names. He'd tackle the Oxford three, he decided; a professor, a physicist and a stockbroker. It would be interesting to find out whether any of them had been in London last Friday. He lifted the phone and began to dial.

At eleven o'clock that morning, Gwen put her head round Hannah's door.

"I've just had a phone call from Adam Greenwood," she said, "wanting to know if I can 'spare him five minutes'."

"Did he say what it was about?" Hannah asked curiously.

"No, but it can't be the broadcast, because his researchers have organised everything."

"When's he coming?"

"Any minute; when he learned I was free, he said he'd be straight over."

"We'll soon know, then."

Gwen's only previous meeting with Adam Greenwood had been a fleeting one at the television studios twelve days ago. Though Mia had been a pupil at Ashbourne for several years, all contact had been with her mother, and this practice had continued after Mrs Perry's second marriage.

When her secretary showed him into her room, she was momentarily surprised how tall he was. He came forward with a smile and shook her hand.

"Good of you to fit me in, Mrs Cameron; I appreciate it."

"So how can I help you, Mr Greenwood?" she asked, motioning him to be seated.

"I was wondering if I might ask a favour, and felt it would be easier in person rather than over the phone."

"Yes?"

Adam leaned back and crossed his legs. "I presume the girls will be attending the broadcast?"

"Most certainly; they're looking forward to it enormously."

He hesitated. "The fact is that for personal reasons, I'd prefer my stepdaughter not to be present."

Gwen looked at him in amazement. "Mia? Why ever not?"

"She's easily embarrassed, as I'm sure you know, and it would be uncomfortable for her to be sitting with her friends while I'm in the spotlight, as it were. Added to which, she was considerably upset after the unfortunate episode last week. You were told about it?"

"Yes, but your wife said she'd recovered quickly, and I must say she's shown no sign of distress. In fact, she seems to have settled in better this term; perhaps it's helped to have her cousin with her." Gwen hesitated. "Does the ban extend to Rebecca?"

"It might be diplomatic, in the circumstances."

Gwen thought for a moment. "Suppose they sat with your family instead of their class?" she suggested. "Then they wouldn't feel so conspicuous, but could still take part in the broadcast, which I'm sure will be educational."

"Unfortunately my family won't be coming," Adam said briskly, adding with a smile, "Six programmes are a lot to expect them to sit through. So – would it be possible for Mia to be given leave of absence from the end of lessons on Thursday, and return with Rebecca the next morning? I appreciate it's bending the rules, but I'd be extremely grateful."

He really left her little choice, Gwen thought resentfully. But a small dispensation was better than risking unpleasantness, which, she felt sure, would follow if Adam Greenwood were thwarted.

"Very well," she said stiffly.

"That's extremely good of you." Having achieved his purpose, Adam was at his most charming. "And if I haven't quite used up my time slot, would it be possible to have a quick look at the hall?"

Gwen glanced at the timetable on the wall. "Yes, we could manage that; no one's using it at the moment."

Scattering hairpins, she led him down the corridor to the

Queen's Hall, ignoring the interest they were attracting from passing girls and staff, and pushed open the swing doors.

"It will be available after Assembly on Thursday, as I told your researchers," she informed him. "I understand that will give everyone sufficient time to set things up."

Adam went past her into the large room, looking about him at the rich panelling, the gallery with tiered seating rising towards the vaulted ceiling, and finally the stage, an impressive focal point with an arching proscenium decorated with frescos and a backcloth of deeply swathed curtains in blue velvet. A heavy oak table was set centre stage, with three chairs behind it.

"What a wonderful setting," he exclaimed.

Gwen glanced at him. "You've not been here before, Mr Greenwood? This is where we hold our end-of-term activities, including Speech Day and the Carol Concert."

"I'm afraid I've been rather remiss; I shall make an effort to attend in future."

After she had shown him out, Gwen returned to Hannah's room.

"Adam Greenwood doesn't want his family here on Thursday," she announced, walking in after a brief tap on the door. Hannah looked up from her desk and the cat, dozing on the window sill in the sunshine, raised its head and blinked sleepily.

"How do you mean?"

"He's asked for Mia to be sent home with Rebecca, and for both of them to stay there."

"Whatever reason did he give?"

"That Mia would be embarrassed to see him holding forth – which is probably true – and that Rebecca's absence would make Mia's less noticeable. As to his family, he says they can't be expected to attend all six programmes."

"He has a point, I suppose. Did you agree about Mia?"

"I more or less had to. Honestly, Hannah, I shall be glad when this pantomime is over."

"Pantomime?" Hannah echoed with raised eyebrow. "What

price the high profile of Ashbourne hosting a quincentenary programme on TV?"

"Yes, well I hadn't thought it through, the disruption to the whole school, with camera, sound and lighting crews tramping around and Lord knows what else. The girls are already un-settled, and we've two more days to go."

"Forget about it," Hannah advised. "Our only responsibility is to ensure that the girls are in their places on time. The rest – all the palaver of cameras and lights and interviews – is their worry, not ours."

"On the contrary, at least one of the interviews is very much my worry," Gwen reminded her. "Don't forget I have to under-go one myself at the end of the programme. I've seen our friend's interviewing techniques, and I'm not relishing the pro-spect."

"You'll do it superbly," Hannah assured her with a smile. "You always do."

Partly mollified, Gwen turned to go. "Do you think Adam Greenwood always gets his own way?" she asked wryly.

"Indubitably," Hannah replied.

The first two Oxford interviews were disappointing. Dr Lane admitted to having known Piers Lester, as did Professor Reid, and it transpired, when asked about their movements that final day, that both had attended Greenwood's party. But in what Webb was coming to regard as the Broadshire tradition, both claimed to have had no contact with their friends since they came down.

"Is this usual, do you suppose, Ken?" Webb demanded, when they had left the imposing portals of St John's College. "Not having been to uni myself, I wouldn't know."

"Me neither, Guv. You'd think, though, even if there were no official reunions, at least a few of them would have come across one another in the normal course of things."

"My thought exactly. They were pretty vague about their

doings last Friday, too. Nothing that could be corroborated, you notice."

"Swore blind they hadn't been to London, though."

"Indeed, but we'll be checking on that. So, two down and one to go. Who have we got left?"

"Martin Edgworth. Lives out at Woodstock."

"Let's hope it's third time lucky, then."

At least they were met with less reserve than they were becoming used to. Edgworth was of medium height with curly brown hair and bright eyes behind horn-rimmed spectacles.

"This must be a thankless task," he greeted them genially. "Come in and take the weight off your feet."

He lived in a seventeenth-century farmhouse on the edge of the village, which, unlike the Kings' country home, had been lovingly renovated in accordance with its period. The result was delightful. Bending his head to go through the low doorway, Webb looked round the small sitting room with pleasure. This was much more to his taste than the grandiose homes of Painswick and Lytton.

"No doubt it's this confounded Lester boy you've come about," Edgworth began, sitting back and crossing his legs. "Shouldn't speak ill of the dead and all that, but honestly, he was a pain in the arse when alive and here he is, still causing trouble all these years after."

A refreshingly different approach, Webb conceded. "What had you against him, sir?"

"He was always pushing himself forward, trying to wangle invitations and gatecrashing parties – that kind of thing. And he'd the hide of a rhinoceros. Most people would get the message that they weren't wanted, but not him."

"Did he have any friends?"

"Not really, though to hear him talk, you'd think he was top of the pops."

"Girls?"

Edgworth grinned. "The only one I recall was the dreaded

186

Carla, property – or so he believed – of one Felix Lytton. Pistols at dawn on that one. Oh, not literally," he added hastily, remembering the reason for their visit. "Old Felix was pretty miffed and gave Carla the elbow, but he soon got over it. Not one to bear a grudge, Felix."

"Is there anyone," Webb asked carefully, "who *might* have borne a grudge?"

"To the extent of doing away with him?" Edgworth shook his head. "He was an infernal nuisance, but basically harmless."

"When did you last see him, sir?" Webb asked resignedly, expecting the usual story. But he was wrong; this time they were given a different slant.

"Down in SB, the day he disappeared."

Webb leant forward. "Morning or afternoon?"

"Afternoon, around five. Said he was stocking up with booze to take to a couple of parties."

Five o'clock. After tea in the refectory, then. Could this be the last sighting of Lester?

"Did he say which parties he was going to?"

"Not in my hearing. All I was concerned about was that he wouldn't show up at the one I was going to, and thankfully he didn't."

"Adam Greenwood's?" Webb suggested.

Edgworth laughed. "Lord no. I wasn't in with that mob. Much too rarefied for me."

"Really? Thought themselves a cut above the rest?"

"Most definitely. We all slopped around in jeans and they looked as though they'd come from Savile Row. Went to poetry readings and such."

Interesting. "And how many were there in this – mob?"

"Twelve. The Twelve Apostles, they called themselves – but in a highly secular sense, I assure you."

"All men?"

"Yes, though they had their camp followers, of course."

187

"Can you remember their names, sir?"

Edgworth looked surprised. "Well – some, I suppose. It's a hell of a time ago, you know."

"It would be helpful if you could try."

"Let's see, then. That final year we rented houses in and around the town, and the Apostles had three between them, four to a house. One lot were just down the road from us. There was Adam, and that chap who's now an MP – Jeremy Painswick – and Greg Blaise." He paused. "The fourth escapes me, I'm afraid."

"And what of the others?" Webb prompted.

"Ah, that's not so easy. Matthew Henderson – he was one of them. You might have read his books – gripping stuff. And Felix Lytton, and Patrick Lane." He frowned, thought for a moment, then shook his head. "That's about all I can remember. I didn't know any of them that well."

Webb thought of the unforthcoming professor they'd left a little earlier. "Justin Reid?" he hazarded.

Edgworth slapped his thigh. "Well done, Superintendent! Yes, he was another. How did you come up with him?"

"What about Nicholas King?"

Edgworth sobered abruptly. "God, yes, poor old Nicholas. Always did seem to be on a knife-edge. Life must have got too much for him."

"Had you seen him recently?"

"My wife and I went to a concert a few months ago, and he invited us backstage. Brilliant, it was."

"How about more recently? Last Friday, for instance, in London?"

Edgworth shook his head. "Sorry, no. As it happens, I *was* in London last Friday, but I didn't see Nicholas. I was tied up in a meeting all day."

"What about your other university friends; seen any of them since you left?"

"Oh Lord yes, we keep in touch. There are reunions and so on,

188

and several of us meet regularly for a drink or a meal. Never discuss Piers Lester, though, if that's what you're wondering."

Webb and Jackson exchanged glances. A normal reaction at last. Then why, when other graduates had continued their friendships, had the Twelve Apostles, allegedly so close at university, cut all ties with each other?

They took their leave of Martin Edgworth and, seeing an attractive-looking pub on the outskirts of the village, stopped for lunch. Jackson placed their order and came over to the table with two brimming glasses. Webb took one with absent-minded thanks. He was obviously deep in thought and they sat in silence for a while, until Jackson finally ventured, "So what do you make of these Apostles, then, Guv?"

Webb sighed and lifted his glass. "I don't know, Ken. I just wish I had all their names; what's so frustrating is that they'll be among those interviewed at the time, but we've no way of winkling them out from the rest. Come to think of it, since they seem to have lived up to their high opinion of themselves, they're probably on my VIP list, but again, which are they?"

"Try asking them all if they've kept in touch."

Their number was called, and Jackson returned to the bar to collect their plates. As he set them down, Webb continued, as though there'd been no interruption: "According to Edgworth, we have Greenwood, Lytton, Painswick, Lane and Reid – all of whom I've interviewed – Blaise, now deceased, and Matthew Henderson, who lives in France. We know from Greenwood that Andrew North was the fourth in his house, and finally there's Nicholas King. Those nine are confirmed as Apostles."

He reached for the mustard. "Which leaves three more. When we get back, we'll check whether any of that lot belong to the Cicero Club, because if I'm not mistaken that was the real reason Greenwood went to the Smoke last Friday; the BBC visit was just a blind."

"You reckon there was a meeting of some kind?"

"Yes, and what's more, I'm willing to bet Nicholas King was there. That, I'm damn sure, is where Greenwood saw him, not some chance encounter on the street, as he'd have us believe.

"Ironically enough," he added, "it was on Friday that I was trying to contact the London-based names, and none were available. Perhaps they were all at the Cicero Club. But even if there wasn't a meeting, Ken, it's surely stretching coincidence that after twenty-seven years of not seeing each other, three of the Apostles are known to have had at least passing contact with each other that day. After which, let's not forget, King topped himself."

"If there *was* a meeting, it must have been something pretty important to bring them together. What do you reckon?"

Webb shrugged. "The discovery of the bones?"

"But why should that have spooked them? Even if they do know something about Lester's vanishing act, nothing linked them with it at the time. Surely there's even less likelihood now."

"Yep, that's what's bugging me. There must be more to it than that."

They ate their meal, their minds circling round the enigmatic Apostles. "We'll have another shot at tracing their movements on Friday," Webb said finally, laying down his knife and fork. "Oxford railway and coach stations, for a start, though ten to one if they did go to London they'd have driven up, and separately, at that. But if we could only break their alibis we might have something to go on."

On returning to his office, Webb rang DI Ledbetter, whom he'd spoken to briefly after the discovery of King's body.

"Dave! I was wondering how things were going. It's been pretty quiet here, I must say."

Webb filled him in with details of the London and Oxford interviews and his growing suspicions about the so-called Apostles.

"Interesting," Ledbetter commented. "The tutor, Pemberton,

mentioned a 'gang', which he later qualified as a group of élitist young men who went around together."

"That would be them, all right. What did he say about them?"

"Nothing much; it was when he was trying to remember who'd had the fight with Lester."

"Did he mention any names, Chris? I know it'll be in your report, but they wouldn't have seemed significant when I read it."

"Hold on a sec, I've got it somewhere, if I can just lay my hands it." There was the sound of shuffling papers, then Ledbetter's voice again. "Yes, here we are: the men Pemberton referred to were Matthew Henderson, Jeremy Painswick MP, Adam Greenwood and Felix Lytton."

All of whom he already knew about, Webb thought, disappointed. "No one else?"

"Afraid not. Do you want me to have another word with him?"

"That would be great, Chris. He mightn't remember any others, but if he did, it would save a lot of hassle."

At six o'clock that evening, Hannah set out to drive to Honeyford. Her phone call earlier, enquiring after Pamela, had resulted in a pressing invitation to supper, Paula insisting her twin would love to see her.

Hannah herself was less sure, being in the invidious position not only of having found the body of Pamela's husband, but of not having liked him in the first place, both factors which would add to the awkwardness inherent in any condolence visit.

Honeyford, which, though only ten miles from Shillingham, she had not visited since she cat-sat for Paula three years ago, looked much as she remembered it, except that trees and shrubs were still clothed in the pale new green of spring rather than the lushness of high summer.

She drove past the Swan, and Swing-Gate Lane, where Dr Pratt lived, and turned up Church Lane, following its loop round to Wychwood, the little cottage which had been her home for three traumatic weeks. And amazingly, Arthur the tabby sat on the gatepost as though awaiting her. It was because she'd fallen for Arthur that on her return from Honeyford Hannah had bought her marmalade kitten.

She got out of the car quickly. "Arthur?" she said.

His ears pricked and he turned his head, amber eyes gazing at her. Then, to show his independence, he proceeded to wash his chest with great deliberation before jumping down and strolling over to her, tail aloft and waving gently. Hannah bent to stroke him and he wound himself round her legs with a purr of welcome.

"You *do* remember me!" she said softly, and, his dignity notwithstanding, scooped him up and hugged him before returning him gently to the ground and moving towards the gate, accompanied by her greeter.

Paula opened the door as she approached it, and gave her a quick hug. "Thanks for coming, Hannah," she said in a low voice. "It will do Pammy good to see a new face."

Pamela herself rose to her feet as Hannah and Paula went into the living room and, as Hannah kissed her, held her close for a long minute. Hannah could feel her trembling, but her voice was quite steady as she said, "Thank you for the beautiful flowers, Hannah. They're gorgeous."

"I'm so very sorry, Pammy."

"Yes." Pamela drew a long, tremulous breath. "I want you to tell me everything. What Nicholas said on the phone, why he wanted to meet you, *exactly* what you found at the cottage."

Hannah made a small movement of protest, but Pamela put a hand up. "Really. It will help, I promise. It's the not knowing which is so hard."

As Paula handed round glasses, Hannah looked from one sister to the other. They weren't identical, Pamela being slightly taller and slimmer than her twin, and her hair, expertly cut in Mayfair, gave her a more sophisticated air than Paula with her shock of dark curls. But both had oval faces and large brown eyes, and their voices were indistinguishable from each other.

Realising that she must submit to the inevitable, Hannah opened the questioning herself. "Had Nicholas seemed upset before he left home?"

Pamela clasped her glass between both hands. "Yes, but I don't know why. It all came on so suddenly; on the Tuesday evening we'd been out to dinner, and he was fine. But the next morning he received a letter, and from then on he seemed to be on edge. He wouldn't tell me who the letter was from, or what was in it, and later that day he had a phone call which he was also secretive about."

Pamela smiled painfully. "I was beginning to wonder if there was a woman involved."

"Did he – keep to his normal routine?" She was doing David's job for him, Hannah thought.

"He went to the music room as usual, but he didn't play. I kept listening, but there was total silence. Thursday was no better, and on Friday he announced that he was going into town to meet someone. I asked who, but he shook his head and said it was no one I knew. When I tried to persist, he flew off the handle and shouted it was none of my business, and why couldn't I leave him alone."

Her voice cracked and she bit her lip. "I hoped whoever it was would soothe him down, but when he came home he was worse than ever. He went straight upstairs, threw some things into a case, and said he was going down to the cottage to sort out a few things. I took my own case out, but he stopped me, insisting he needed to be alone. Then he – he took me in his arms and held me so tightly I could hardly breathe. And told me he loved me."

She stopped speaking and in the quiet room her quick breathing was an indication of her fight for control.

"Tell Hannah about the note," Paula said softly.

Pamela looked up, her eyes haunted. "It was a standard

suicide one – no explanation at all. He simply said he loved me and hoped I'd forgive him, but he couldn't take any more."

She set the glass down suddenly and covered her face with both hands. "He might have given me a reason!" she cried. "Couldn't he see what it would do to me, not knowing *why*?"

Paula went to her quickly, kneeling beside her and putting her arms round her. Hannah got up and walked to the french windows, looking down the walled garden she remembered. The other two cats were lying on the warm path, basking in the last of the evening sunshine.

Behind her, she heard the sisters stir and Paula return to her chair. Pamela blew her nose. "Sorry," she said. "Now, Hannah, please tell me all you know."

Hannah turned back. "I wish there was more. He rang up out of the blue on Friday evening and said he needed to see me urgently. I was afraid you were ill or something, but he said no, though it was because I was your friend that he was ringing."

"Because you were my friend?"

"Yes. I – half wondered, like you, if there was someone else, if he wanted me to tell you he was leaving. But I couldn't see him that evening because I already had an engagement, and I suggested he came into Shillingham the next morning."

"What did he say?"

"He was adamant that I must go out there." Hannah hesitated. "Pamela, I can't stop thinking that if I *had* gone—"

"No," Pamela cut in quickly, "you're wrong. I'm convinced that he was determined to kill himself and nothing you could have said would have stopped him. He was – obviously saying goodbye to me, though I didn't realise it at the time."

"And that's why he wouldn't agree to go to Shillingham," Paula added. "He meant to kill himself at the cottage, and needed to be sure someone would find him before Pamela came down looking for him."

Which was what David had said.

"I'm sorry, Hannah," Pamela said in a low voice. "It was unforgivable to use you like that."

"He wanted to spare you. That was fair enough."

Pamela sighed. "You were my last chance. I was hoping against hope that something he said might have thrown some light on it. Now, I'll never know."

Hannah hesitated. She longed to comfort her friend by saying that the police were still investigating, that a motive might yet emerge, but she kept silent. Despite their enquiries, nothing might come to light and she would have given Pamela false hope.

"I think we've said all we can on the matter," Paula announced, much to Hannah's relief. "So let's put it behind us now, and have some supper."

They moved to the table under the window, which was ready laid for three, and Paula brought in a large dish of lasagne.

"I believe Adam Greenwood's doing a programme from Ashbourne?" she remarked as she ladled it out. "That's quite an honour, isn't it?"

Hannah launched into Gwen's reservations about the broadcast, making the sisters smile, and the rest of the evening passed without any further reference to the suicide.

It was only as she was driving home that Hannah realised neither Paula nor Pamela had mentioned that Nicholas knew Adam at university. In the circumstances, that struck her as surprising.

When she reached home, she took the lift to the floor beyond her own, and knocked on David's door. He opened it with a glass of whisky in his hand.

"Come in. I'm relaxing after a long and frustrating day."

"Not making any progress?" she asked, as he took her coat and gestured her into the living room.

"Not that you'd notice. A few leads, but all very tenuous. What have you been doing with yourself?"

"Adam Greenwood came to school today."

"Ah."

"I didn't see him, but he told Gwen he didn't want Mia to be at the broadcast, and that his family wouldn't be there, either."

Webb frowned. "Seems a bit odd, doesn't it?"

"He said she'd be embarrassed, which she probably would, and that the family couldn't be expected to attend all six Shillingham broadcasts. All the same, he managed to get Gwen's back up. She'll be glad when it's over."

Hannah accepted the glass he handed her and sat down. "And this evening I've been to Honeyford to see Pamela King."

"Oh, she's there, is she? No wonder Wimbledon drew a blank. How's she bearing up?"

"Trying to put a brave face on it." Hannah smiled. "I did a bit of snooping on your behalf."

"Good for you. Find out anything?"

"She said Nicholas was fine until the Wednesday morning, when he received a letter which upset him."

"That's interesting. Who from?"

"He wouldn't say, nor what was in it. And later that day there was a phone call, which he wouldn't discuss either."

"Was he always this secretive?"

"I doubt it. Then on the Friday he announced he was going into town to meet someone."

"To meet someone?" Webb repeated sharply. "Who?"

"No idea, but when he came home he was in a terrible state. Went straight upstairs and packed his bags, said he was coming down here but wouldn't let Pamela come with him. Then he held her tightly and told her he loved her." Hannah's eyes fell. "She thinks now he was saying goodbye to her. And there was something else, David, which only struck me just now, in the car. We were talking about Adam's broadcast, but neither of the twins mentioned the fact that Nicholas had known him. Yet he must have done, mustn't he?"

"Oh yes," Webb said grimly, "they knew each other all right. What's more, they met in London last Friday, though according to Greenwood it wasn't planned. I didn't believe him at the time, and from what you say, it looks as though I was right."

Hannah stared at him. "Is it significant, do you think?"

"It could well be. You've done very well, Inspector James; what you've told me bears out a theory I'm working on, though I'd give a lot to know more about that letter and phone call."

"What's most upsetting Pamela is not knowing why he did it. Is there any hope of your finding out?"

"I'll do my damnedest," Webb promised her.

Fourteen

" Russell – have you seen Adam this morning? I've tried ringing the flat, but there's no reply. Imogen's at work, of course."

"Sorry, Ma, can't help. He's probably sorting out last-minute details for tomorrow."

"That's what I wanted to speak to him about; Verity and I haven't got our tickets yet. I just wanted to make sure there's no hitch."

"Ah."

Eva frowned. "What do you mean, 'Ah'?"

"Adam suggested that we have everyone round here, to watch the programme on the box."

"What? But the girls—"

"That's really it, Ma: he thinks it would be embarrassing for Mia and she'd be better at home. And the rest of us could hardly troop along and leave her by herself."

After a minute, Eva said, "That's a little high-handed, isn't it?"

"You know Adam! Anyway, Louise is providing wine and nibbles, which is all we'll need after eating earlier."

"When was this arranged?" Eva asked, a hint of displeasure in her voice.

"Last night. Imogen and Mia are coming, and I was just about to phone you."

"Elliott will be down, too. I'm meeting him at lunchtime."

"Fine; the more the merrier. And tell Verity Naomi will be welcome, if she'd like to come."

199

"Just as well you've a large sitting room," Eva commented. "Very well, since everything seems to be settled I suppose there's no more to be said. I was looking forward to seeing the school, though."

"There'll be plenty of other chances," Russell assured her.

Earlier that morning, Webb had found a handwritten envelope on his desk, marked 'Personal'. To his astonishment it contained two tickets for the Ashbourne broadcast, with the scrawled pencil comment, *I think you might find this interesting. AG.*

He pulled the phone towards him and rang Steeple Bayliss. "Chris? Guess what? Greenwood has sent me two tickets for his show tomorrow!"

"Good God! Does he regard you as a fan?"

"Says I might find it interesting. Would you care to join me?"

"You bet I would, but isn't there some dolly-bird you'd rather take?"

Webb smiled to himself at this totally erroneous description of Hannah – who, in any case, would be there in an official capacity. "I'm fresh out of dolly-birds," he said. "Come over about seven and we'll have a bite to eat first."

"Fine, thanks. As it happens, I was just going to give you a buzz. I went back to Pemberton, as you asked, and after a lot of thought he came up with a couple more names, James Meredith, who is some sort of research fellow down at Exeter, and the film director Chester Van Hoek, of all people."

Whom Fleming had mentioned, Webb remembered.

"If you're thinking of flying out to Hollywood," Ledbetter continued, a grin in his voice, "remember it was me who put you on to him!"

"He's on my VIP list," Webb replied, "but I didn't know he was one of the Twelve."

"You sound positively biblical, old son! What about Meredith? Is he on your list, too?"

"No; it seems the Old Man doesn't set so much store by Fellows."

"In that case I'll nip down to Exeter and have a word, though no doubt he'll be as tight-lipped as the others."

"I keep hoping that as the pressure builds, one of them will crack. Good hunting, Chris."

"Sonia? Adam here."

Sonia sat down suddenly on the arm of a chair. "Hello, Adam. How are you?"

"Fine, fine. I never really thanked you for the TLC last week. It was very good of you."

"Not at all."

There was a slight pause. Then, "Will you be watching the broadcast tomorrow evening?"

"I should think so." No need to tell him she never missed his programmes.

"Please try to, and the children too. It'll be – quite instructive."

She raised an eyebrow. Since when had Adam shown any interest in his children's instruction?

"It covers five hundred years of education," he added, when she made no comment. "What about William? Will he be with you?"

"No, he's only just gone back." As Adam must know.

"No chance of his sneaking home for a night?"

"To watch a TV programme? None whatever, but don't worry, I'm sure there's the odd set in Swindon."

Surely this was carrying egomania too far, even for Adam. What did it matter if William saw his broadcast or not?

"Would you pass on the message, then?"

"That you want him to watch you?" she asked incredulously.

"I'd like him to, yes." Adam's voice was clipped. "It's not much to ask, is it?"

"I suppose not, though he should be working."

"Thanks, Sonia, I'd appreciate it. I'll – be in touch." And he rang off.

With a disbelieving shake of her head, Sonia, who was spending her free day working on the pageant costumes, returned to her sewing machine.

Verity had spent the day in Steeple Bayliss, visiting friends she'd known when they lived there, and Eva had trailed round auction rooms with Elliott all afternoon. Both women were tired and were relaxing with pre-dinner drinks when Eva mentioned the arrangements for the next day.

"So it seems Adam has organised our evening for us," she finished. "Though why we can't all watch it on our own sets as we did last week, heaven knows."

"Well, since Naomi's included in the invitation, I'll give her a ring. She's feeling a bit down at the moment – it'll do her good to have some company."

"You know," Eva mused, "much as I love having Adam here, I'll be glad when he goes back to London. I can't help feeling that Broadshire poses some kind of . . . threat to him. Things haven't been right ever since he arrived."

"Are we back to the Twelve Apostles?"

Eva sighed. "I suppose so, yes. Oh, Verity, if only you hadn't happened to be on the spot when Mr Morrison was killed! Then, even if it *was* Adam's Apostles he was referring to, at least we shouldn't have known about it."

The next morning, Webb detailed Simon Marshbanks to go through the list of potential Apostles and other VIPs and check whether any of them belonged to the Cicero Club. And at last they were rewarded: after a quick knock on Webb's door, Simon erupted into the room.

"Got it, Guv!" he exclaimed excitedly. "Andrew North – one of your VIPs. Professor of History at Cambridge, blah-blah-blah. Several clubs listed, including the Cicero!"

"Well done, Simon!" Webb took the book from him and read the entry. North, with a string of initials after his name, had been born in Edinburgh and educated at Fettes College and Broadshire University. His present occupation was listed as Professor of History and fellow of Queens' College, Cambridge – some two hundred miles away.

Webb looked at his watch. Already gone eleven; it would be cutting it fine to set out now and be back in time for tonight's broadcast, which he was loath to miss. However, interviewing North was top priority.

As it happened, the quandary was resolved for him. Professor North, he was informed, was out of town for the next few days. Perhaps Mr Webb could call back next week? Declining to leave a message – no point in putting the man on his guard – Webb rang off, swearing under his breath.

He was impatient, now, to come to grips with the Apostles, and the Cicero Club seemed his best chance. It was fair to assume that North had hosted the meeting last Friday, when Greenwood at least had paid the club a visit. How many others had entered those prestigious portals, and for what purpose? It seemed Webb had no option but to cool his heels till the professor returned to base.

He took out his VIP list. Now that Pemberton had named another two Apostles, only one member was outstanding. Was his name on this list? Impossible to guess. Everyone here would have to be seen, and with at least three resident abroad, that could be tricky.

The phone rang – Ledbetter, reporting on his visit to Exeter. "Sorry not to come back to you yesterday, Dave; it took me some time to reach Meredith. He was cloistered away till nearly five o'clock and couldn't be disturbed. Then, when I did nab him, he wasn't very receptive. The story much as before, I'm afraid. Yes, he vaguely knew Lester at university; no, he'd no idea what had happened to him, though he'd heard, of course, that his remains had been discovered. And – guess what? He's seen neither hair nor hide of any of his pals since the end of that last term."

"Par for the course," commented Webb. "What kind of bloke is he?"

"Typical boffin. Pale, intense, thick spectacles, living on a different planet."

Webb smiled. "I'm sure he liked you, too! Well, at least it's another interview we can tick off. See you later."

At Ashbourne, there had been an undercurrent of excitement all day. As soon as Assembly was over the television crews had moved in, weaving around each other with practised ease as they set up their individual equipment.

Mia, who'd been told of her stepfather's wishes, had concurred without comment, albeit surprised by his consideration. The chief bonus, though, was that spending the evening at Greenwood meant that she'd see Tom, who'd been sending her notes via Rebecca for the past week. The arrangement suited her very well.

Imogen had also been surprised at her husband's decision, having fully expected to attend this broadcast. Nor did she particularly wish to spend the evening with her in-laws, though there was no way that she could see to avoid it. And it *was* good of Adam to consider Mia's feelings.

About Adam himself, she was still concerned. Last night he'd hardly slept at all; she'd woken to see him standing at the window staring into the darkness, but he'd refused her offer to make tea. After telling her to go back to sleep he'd left the room, presumably to avoid disturbing her further. Nor did he return until nearly seven, when he went straight to the bathroom for a shower.

Once this broadcast was over, she intended to persuade him to see a doctor. That something was seriously wrong she no longer doubted, and the worry gnawed like a worm in her stomach.

"Everything all right?" Christina enquired, coming upon her staring pensively out of the window.

Imogen snapped to. "Fine, thanks."

"I'm looking forward to this evening."

"This evening?"

"The broadcast. Everyone's been invited – all the parents, I mean. Didn't you know?"

Imogen shook her head. "Actually, we're opting out this time and watching it on the box."

Christina looked at her in disbelief. "You're not serious? But *why*, for heaven's sake? I'd have thought this was one you'd be sure not to miss, with Mia at Ashbourne and everything."

Unable to think of a plausible reply, Imogen merely smiled and Christina, puzzled, let the matter drop.

Everything was going according to schedule; the outside-broadcast unit and make-up caravan were *in situ*, while in the Queen's Hall the stage and part of the auditorium had been converted into a replica of Adam's famous London studio, complete with its huge back-projection screen on which the programme would be relayed as it progressed. For the convenience of those farther back, a series of monitors had been fixed to the carved pillars down each side.

The girls had already filed in and taken their places in the gallery, leaving the body of the hall for their parents and other guests, and the room was now filled with a murmur of anticipation. There'd been no pre-show hospitality, but a buffet was laid out in the dining hall for after the programme.

The front few rows of seats had been reserved on the far side of the aisle for the heads of schools from all over the county, members of the local education committee and the Mayor and Mayoress.

On the near side, Hannah was sitting with Bruce Cameron, the school governors and their partners, ostensibly chatting to her neighbours while ticking off a mental checklist and keeping an eye on arrivals, who were being greeted by Gwen at the door.

David had phoned last night to warn her he'd be putting in an appearance. She'd not seen him come in, but then she'd been busy with her guests. And now it seemed everyone had arrived; the doors were closed, Gwen was returning to her seat, and the floor manager on stage embarked on his briefing routine. The show was about to begin.

Adam Greenwood's appearance was greeted with enthusiastic applause. He gave a brief resumé of Ashbourne's history for the benefit of the television audience, outlined the format the programme would be following, and introduced his first guest, the woman historian who'd appeared with him the previous week.

As she launched into a description of education in the fifteenth century, Hannah's attention was distracted by Adam's uncharacteristic fidgeting. Something was wrong, she thought, studying him uneasily; his face was flushed and his eyes were continually scanning the audience. She wondered if he was looking for anyone in particular.

Hannah glanced sideways at Gwen, but her attention was fixed on the speaker, and from her relaxed posture Hannah deduced that she'd not noticed anything amiss. Perhaps it was her imagination; but surely he didn't usually take so many sips of water from the glass provided? After all, he was used to the lights, and had not previously shown any signs of discomfort.

She forced her attention back to Miss Derringer, whose interview was being illustrated by slides of old schoolrooms, children in period dress, and the first, rudimentary methods of instructing them. Dutifully, Hannah gazed at the huge screen, but the images didn't register.

Suppose Adam were taken ill, what should they do? Oh God, if this had to happen, why couldn't it have been at one of the other venues? There weren't even any members of his family present.

A succession of guests followed one after another as the programme progressed inexorably down the centuries. Would Adam keep going to the end? Hannah wondered. And was she the only one to notice all was not well? His discomfiture must surely be visible to the entire audience, magnified as it was by the huge image on the back-projection screen. Yet Charles Frobisher on her right seemed as oblivious as Gwen, clapping enthusiastically as the latest guest left the stage.

I'm not going to remember a word of this, Hannah thought helplessly. She'd been looking forward to the broadcast, but now all she wanted was for it to be over. Too bad it was live and couldn't be watched with more attention later. To add to her frustration, in all the rush of getting ready she'd forgotten to set her video-recorder.

Her attention was recalled by Gwen's movements preparatory to going on stage for the final interview. Thank God! If Adam could last only a few minutes more, it would be safely over.

Forcing herself to concentrate, Hannah listened as Gwen replied succinctly and eruditely to Adam's questions on education today, and went on to outline some of the developments envisaged for the future. It was, Hannah thought proudly, an excellent summing-up with which to end the programme.

In thanking Gwen, Adam announced to the wider audience that Mrs Cameron would shortly be leaving Ashbourne to take up an appointment in Canada, and congratulated her on the high standards the school had maintained under her headship.

It was over! Hannah breathed a sigh of relief as, clapping hard, she watched Gwen descend the steps and return to her seat. As soon as Adam had wound up the show, she would slip away to check that the buffet was in readiness.

He held up his hand for silence, but as the applause died away the expected closing comments were not forthcoming.

"Ladies and gentlemen," he began instead, "I hope you will

forgive me if I encroach on your time a little longer. There is a statement I wish to make, and this seems the ideal opportunity."

There was a surprised stirring as the audience, preparing to take their leave, settled back in their seats. Adam glanced briefly at his floor manager. "I warned my producer we'd overrun by about ten minutes. I'm not sure if the cameras will keep rolling – that's up to the network controllers – but what I have to say will make national headlines."

He sat down again, seeming, to Hannah's surprise, more at ease than he'd been all evening. Perhaps he'd been bracing himself for what was coming.

"What you're about to hear, ladies and gentlemen, is a confession. It's over twenty years too late – and for that, I'm more sorry than I can say – and it relates to events which took place at Broadshire University in 1972. Over the last week, I've learned that what happened that evening has been weighing heavily on the consciences of all concerned, but no one felt able to make a move. Because, you see, it wasn't an individual guilt, which any one of us could have admitted to, but a communal one.

"Now, however, we're agreed the truth must come out, and since we all live our lives to some extent in the public eye, it seems appropriate to make the announcement publicly."

Conscious that he had the undivided attention of everyone in the hall, Adam took another sip of water and settled back in his chair.

"You will all know that the remains of Piers Lester, who disappeared twenty-seven years ago, have just been uncovered. I have to tell you that his parents, Sir Digby and Lady Lester, are in the audience this evening at my express invitation. So are several of my university colleagues, many of whose names will be familiar to you.

"So if you will bear with me, I should like to tell you for the first time exactly what happened on the last evening of Trinity term that year."

God! Hannah thought, her heart racing. I hope David managed to get here!

"At the time," Adam was continuing, "I was one of a group of rather pretentious young men, who deliberately cultivated an air of exclusivity and fought off all attempts by other students to amalgamate with us, Piers Lester among them.

"That last evening, as you can imagine, there were leaving parties all around the town. We – the Twelve Apostles, as we called ourselves – had limited ours to just ourselves and our girlfriends, since it was the last foreseeable occasion we'd all be together. And as was regrettably the custom at student parties – and probably still is – drugs were circulating."

A caption flashed onto the screen behind him, below the huge image of his face: *The next programme will follow shortly.* They were still on air, then.

If he was aware of this, Adam gave no sign. "The party was in full swing when Piers gatecrashed – already, it has to be said, the worse for drink. Frankly, though, by that time we were too laid back to care, and allowed him help himself to speed like everyone else. No one seems to have noticed when he left the room, but a couple of hours later someone went up to the bathroom and found him lying on the floor." Adam paused. "He was dead, having apparently choked on his own vomit."

There was total silence throughout the hall.

Adam went on, his calm voice reflecting none of the drama of his words. "The alarm was raised, and while two of us frantically tried to revive him, the girls were bundled out of the house and taken home. I must stress here that none of them had any idea what had happened, either then or later.

"Needless to say, our first-aid attempts were useless, and when the others returned from seeing the girls home, we discussed what best to do. Of *course* we should have reported it, but, quite simply, we panicked. Piers had died after taking drugs in our house, and although we were originally going to leave him

209

somewhere where he'd be found, we were afraid that the drugs in his body might be traced back to us. So – unforgiveably – we decided to bury him. My car was parked outside. We managed to get him into it, and three of us drove him out to Fox Woods."

Adam looked down at his intent audience, his face sombre. "We can never make up to Sir Digby and Lady Lester for their years of anguish. If it's any comfort, he was given as Christian a burial as we could manage, and some prayers were said at the graveside. By the next day the whole thing seemed unbelievable, a bad dream. We were about to disperse all over the country, and the twelve of us made a solemn vow not to divulge what had happened, nor attempt to contact each other in any way. Which, believe it or not, we held to until last week."

Adam took another sip of water. "But by then, two things had happened; one of our number, Gregory Blaise, had died of cancer, and, by a strange quirk of fate, within days of his death, Piers's grave was discovered. Both events were a shock, but we'd always known the grave would be found one day, and it could hardly point to us after all this time.

"Greg's death, though, had profound consequences, because as the end drew near, he couldn't bear the guilt any longer and confided in his parish priest, the Reverend Eric Morrison.

"Which, as you'll appreciate, shifted the burden on to Mr Morrison, whose immediate concern was that Sir Digby and his wife should be told. But as he couldn't betray Greg's confidence, his hands were tied. Perhaps Greg had guessed that we, too, were ready to own up; at any rate, he gave Morrison our names and addresses, and suggested he contact us personally, with a view to our agreeing to set the record straight.

"I happened to be first on the list, so, two weeks ago, he came here to Shillingham and attended the first of these broadcasts. Afterwards he came to my dressing room and tried to persuade me to come forward, arguing that Lester's death had, after all, been an accident.

"I'm ashamed to say, though, that suddenly discovering an outsider knew the truth threw me completely, and I refused point-blank to discuss it. But Morrison didn't give up; the next morning he wrote to me, setting out the arguments I'd not given him time to make, and saying he'd written to the other members of the group, but was holding back the letters till he'd spoken to me. He delivered my letter to the studio, but, ironically enough, was fatally injured soon afterwards in a road accident.

"When I heard of his death, I regret to say that I hoped that was the end of the matter. It wasn't, of course; his letter was waiting for me when I next went to the studio."

Adam passed a hand over his forehead, the first overt sign of strain since he'd begun speaking. "As soon as I read it I knew the outcome was inevitable, and although I was considerably shaken, there was also a great sense of relief.

"I was still wondering what move to make when, a couple of days later, I had a call from a former colleague, who'd just received Morrison's letter. It hadn't occurred to me that his daughter would find the letters and post them, and it was an enormous relief that I wouldn't after all have to contact everyone with lengthy explanations. We agreed that as many of us as possible should meet in London later that week, and in the meantime I would contact the three members of the group who were abroad, tell them the position and ask for their views. This I did, and they each gave me their proxy vote should that be needed.

"So, after a gap of twenty-seven years, eight of us came together, and discovered that despite our successful careers, we'd all been living with a deep sense of guilt which we could see no way of alleviating.

"Unfortunately, though, the decision to confess was not unanimous, Nicholas King fearing that the adverse publicity would end his career. In point of fact, all of us had a lot to lose, and though we tried to persuade him, he insisted that after all this time it was better to leave things as they were. So we were forced to hold the secret ballot which we'd hoped to avoid, and, including the proxy votes, the result was ten to one in favour of confession."

Again Adam paused, before adding flatly, "As you probably know, Nicholas killed himself at the weekend."

He pushed back his chair and rose slowly to his feet. "Now, ladies and gentlemen, I'm going to ask the rest of my colleagues to join me here on the stage. As we agreed, I shall name them as they come up. I should mention that some have flown from halfway round the world to be here this evening and take their share of the blame."

Hannah turned at the sound of scraping chairs. Around the hall men were getting to their feet and coming forward, and as each one climbed the steps to the stage, Adam intoned his name – like, Hannah thought, a memorial service after some disaster.

"Matthew Henderson, who's flown in from France; Felix Lytton; Justin Reid; Jeremy Painswick; Patrick Lane; Andrew North; James Meredith; John Palmer – just arrived from Hong Kong; and Chester Van Hoek, from the United States."

The men stood in line, shoulder to shoulder, stoically facing the audience.

"I also invited Detective Superintendent Webb and a colleague to be present this evening," Adam continued, and, turning again, Hannah saw David at last as he and his companion stood up.

"We'll be waiting for you backstage, Superintendent. And this, ladies and gentlemen, really is the end of the programme. Thank you for your forbearance, and good-night."

The audience, uncertain of protocol in such unimagined circumstances, remained silent, and in that silence the ten remaining members of the Apostles turned and walked, still in line, into the wings and out of sight.

*   *   *

212

The after-show buffet had been a dismal failure; the guests, not knowing each other well enough to discuss what was on all their minds, were eager to get home where they could speak more freely, and most of the food remained untouched.

Gwen and Hannah had spoken briefly, but agreed to postpone any discussion until the morning, when they would have had time to assimilate what had happened. The 'Apostles' were still closeted in one of the classrooms with Webb and his colleague, and the two women thankfully left the security staff to shut up the building and, heads still spinning, returned to their respective homes.

Half an hour later, Hannah's doorbell rang.

"David! You're back earlier than I expected. Come in."

"Well, there's hardly any urgency," Webb said tiredly, sitting down and gratefully accepting the glass she handed him. "Nothing to be gained by rounding up the troops at this time of night to embark on lengthy statement-taking – times ten, at that."

"So what's happened?"

"They've given me their names and phone numbers and I'll contact them individually in the morning. Starting," he added grimly, "with Adam Greenwood. Then they'll be arrested and bailed to come back in two months. Meanwhile I'll compile a report and forward it to the Crown Prosecution Service."

"What's likely to happen to them?"

Webb shrugged. "The CPS will have to decide whether, after all this time, it's in the public interest to do anything about it. They *might* want to make an example of them – perverting the course of justice, offences under the Coroner's Act and all that. Or – and personally I think this is the more likely – they could let them off with the proverbial slap on the wrist. It's not as though they'd killed the boy, after all – the minister was right there. In which case they'd probably get off with probation or a suspended sentence."

"Even the best scenario could ruin their careers," Hannah said, unwittingly echoing Nicholas King.

"Not necessarily," Webb replied judiciously. "It certainly won't harm Adam Greenwood's. His ratings will go sky-high after this, I shouldn't wonder. As for the others, it depends how they carry it off. There'll be plenty of media interest, yes, but in my opinion it'll be a nine days' wonder; if they quietly carry on with their work and keep their heads down, I reckon they'll all survive."

"I hope they do," Hannah said thoughtfully. "It sounds trite to say so, but I think they've suffered enough." She paused. "You saw Sir Digby and his wife? How were they?"

"Shell-shocked is the best description. Lady Lester was in tears, but I'd say they were partly of relief. At last she knows what happened, and that her son wasn't brutally murdered, which I think was what she feared. Once his funeral's over, I'm sure they'll come to terms with it."

He gave a tired grin. "Fortunately the Chief Super was glued to the box tonight, which saved a lot of explanation. Otherwise, I'd still be on the blower. I must say, though, as a confession, it certainly had novelty value. Trust Adam Greenwood to make a production number out of it."

Eva stood at her window looking up at the sky. Though there was no moon, the stars gave the night an overall luminosity and the blurred shapes of trees showed a deeper dark against the sky. Adam had returned some time ago, but he'd gone straight to the flat to Imogen and Mia and she hadn't seen him. Perhaps it was as well, for what could she say?

She let the curtain fall and turned from the window, surveying her bed across the room without interest. Her brain was still far too active to sleep, yet she was exhausted from the endless replaying in her head of Adam's incredible confession. Her worries about the Twelve Apostles had been more than justified.

She jumped as a faint tap came on the door. "Yes?"

The handle turned and Verity appeared in her dressing-gown,

bearing two mugs on a tray. "I saw the light under your door, and thought you might like some hot chocolate."

"Bless you," Eva said quietly. They sat down at the table in the window.

"Are you all right?" Verity asked after a moment.

"I shall be."

Which, Verity thought, was a very 'Eva' reply. "Of course you will. And so will Adam."

"Just imagine, V, living with that secret all these years. No wonder poor Nicholas King cracked." She looked at her friend with a rueful smile. "I was right, wasn't I, about Broadshire being a threat to Adam?"

Verity nodded. "But at least it's not hanging over him any more, and I suppose it could have been worse. As a threat, I mean."

"I'm glad we were all together when we learned about it; it was thoughtful of Adam to arrange that, and a bonus that Elliott was here, too."

"How's his flat coming along? Were you able to find everything he needed?" Elliott and Eva had had another tour of the auction rooms that day.

"Almost, I think." Eva detailed some of their bargains, and Verity was relieved to see the tension begin to drain out of her. She finished her chocolate and got to her feet.

"Well, I won't keep you from your bed any longer, and remember, tomorrow's another day."

Eva nodded smilingly, and Verity let herself out of the room. After a minute Eva also rose and went to her dresser. Taking out the box containing the Apostle spoons, she laid it on her bedside table and slowly lifted the lid. Then, as Verity had done before her, she took out each spoon in turn, her finger tracing the ridges and hollows of the tiny figures before laying them gently back in their satin – graves, she thought suddenly, seeing the indentations in an unwelcome new light.

The ceremony completed, she closed the lid and stood for a

moment with her hand resting on it. This, she knew, had been her farewell to them, for though she would always keep the spoons, she would never use them again.

Putting the box back in the drawer, she covered it with some silk scarves before, with the sense of duty done, climbing at last into her bed.